10/16 CL

MOGZILLA

Paperback edition: ISBN: 9781906132460
Text copyright Paul Nolan
Cover by Rebecca Davy.
Cover ©Mogzilla 2016
Printed in the UK.
First published by Mogzilla in 2016.

Author's dedication:

To Harry

Chapter 1

I was woken by screaming, screams that got louder. A girl lay face down beside me. I pulled her up and she looked at me. She was confused and terrified. That's how I felt too. She turned away and looked back to where the screams were coming from. Hundreds of frightened children were running towards us. I stumbled back, pulling the girl with me. My back crashed into something hard. It was a stone. A stone that stood much taller than me.

An arc of large grey stones stood in front of us. I could see the children through the gaps between the tall stones as thick, black smoke clouds spiraled up behind them. The sky was so dark that it looked like night.

The running children were now so close that I could see the fear on their faces. I grabbed the girl's hand. It was shaking. So was mine. She smiled weakly as the children ran into the middle of the stone circle and stopped. Soon the circle was full of children: some were huddled in groups, others wandered around dazed. Many were crying.

I looked at the girl and she nodded back at me, letting go of my hand. We walked out and joined the children.

Then we saw what had terrified them, what they were running away from. The girl and I linked hands again and screamed with the others.

Shapes rose above the hill and moved towards the circle. Shapes of men sat upon horses. Flames rose from their torches. Their weapons shone in the darkness.

Ahead of the riders were hundreds of marching shadows. As they moved the ground beneath them shook. The blackness began to drain from the sky and the horror became clearer.

Tall warriors strode out of the blackness holding long-handled axes. Flickering flames bounced off their bronze blades. When the army had stopped, the ground lay silent again. Only a lone figure on horseback moved forward. He raised a huge mace above his head and then pointed it towards us. The earth began to shake again as his men charged past him.

The army ran towards us, pushing the girl and I to the back of the circle. We took cover behind a stone. Arrows rattled towards us, scraping our stone shield, sparks bouncing off it as they hit.

The girl holding my hand shouted. She was pointing at another little girl who smiled as she picked up arrows, as if they were flowers in a field. A large boy appeared from behind a stone and began to limp quickly towards the infant. At that moment a wave of arrows flew towards them, darkening the sky.

The boy wasn't going to make it. The arrows were moving much quicker than him. The girl let go of my hand and ran towards the infant, leaping over the fallen stones like a young deer. She reached the little girl before the boy and pulled both of them back towards the cover of the stones. Arrows thudded into the ground all around them. They'd survived the attack and now they were safely back behind the standing stones. The boy wrapped his arms around his rescuer and spoke to her. I had no idea what he said but I guessed he was saying thank you.

But it wasn't over yet. The ground trembled as screaming warriors on horseback charged forward, swinging their weapons above their heads. The boy pulled two daggers from his belt. He gave me the bronze one and kept a stone dagger for himself. The small girl sat scrunched behind the boy, terrified and shaking.

We stood in front of the stones. It was children against men – daggers and stones against maces and axes. I closed my eyes and prayed.

Then I heard a cry. Not from the children in the stone circle. Not from the men galloping on horses. I opened my eyes. The cry came from another advancing army. Hundreds of men and women were charging over the grassy hills towards our attackers. They came at the riders from the left and right throwing spears and waving axes. The horses panicked. Some stopped suddenly, throwing their riders to the ground. Others turned sharply and crashed into the crowd. Horses reared up and weapons clashed.

The enemy were no longer advancing. They were trapped between two walls of warriors. Arrows rained down on them from the mounds above. Bodies began to fall. A loud horn blast silenced their weapons. They ran in the only direction they could – away from us.

A huge cheer spread around the stone circle. The children ran out of the circle almost as quickly as they had run into it. Tears of happiness rolled down their cheeks as they hugged their parents.

Some of the children pointed at us and spoke quietly to their parents. A tall man approached. He had a big, brown animal skin wrapped around his shoulders and he wore two horns around his neck that rattled on his gold chest plate. In his hand he held a huge blue-headed mace.

The men, women and children formed a ring around us. When the man spoke to us I had no idea what he was saying. The people gathered in the circle began to whisper to each other. They looked scared. The man spoke again. When we didn't answer, he began to shout. His anger scared me. He shouted again and four warriors ran up and grabbed us. I threw my arms back but three muscular men held me tight. Their awful smell made my eyes water.

The man with the mace turned to the circle and shouted one word: "Ecron."

The ring of people then began to chant the same word.

"Ec-ron...Ec-RON...EC-RON."

Each time, the chanting got louder. The crowd disappeared behind a cloud of dust that rose from their stamping feet.

A figure appeared out of the dust. Its face was hidden behind a mask of animal skin with huge antlers sticking out of its head. The figure was dressed in a robe of what looked like animal skin patches of different browns. A necklace of teeth hung down from its chest and its arms were covered in animal bones. Ecron was its name.

Ecron drew nearer as the chanting grew louder. It held out its hands and I shuddered as it pulled my mouth open. I tried to bite down but the men stopped me. I tasted the dirt and blood on their fingers. The chanting stopped and a gasp went around the circle. Then Ecron began to feel around the sides of my head. As it moved its crooked fingers, it mumbled. There were only two yellow teeth in its mouth.

Suddenly its head rocked back. Ercon's animal mask had come loose and I could see braided hair covered in blue beads, rattling like a snake. Ecron was a woman. She turned back and shouted something to the crowd. A murmur went around the circle.

Ecron did the same thing to the girl, lifting her arms to the sky and making a circle around her head as she chanted. Everyone copied her. All except the tall boy with a limp and his arrow-picking sister who were both crying.

Ecron moved back as the chief approached us. He held out his mace and spoke to us. Whatever he said wasn't good. The girl sensed it too. She spoke for the first time and I was surprise when I could understand every word she was saying.

"Why are you doing this? We saved your little girl," she said.

The chief stepped back. Ecron moved forward and spoke. As she did, she formed the circle above her head again but moved her arms around quicker this time. The girl turned to me:

"They're going to kill us in the morning if the sun isn't shining. They think that our death will make the sun shine again."

Ecron smiled a toothless grin as she pulled a small pot from beneath her animal skin. The last thing I remember is the awful smell of what was inside it.

Chapter 2

I opened my eyes for a moment then closed them again. Smoke swirled everywhere and stung my eyes. I opened them again, this time for a little longer but everything was hidden by the thick smoke. My hands were tied. My ankles were tied too. The ropes cut into me when I moved.

I sat still on the hard floor and listened. There was a fire close by. I could hear its crackle and feel its warmth. There was no breeze. The room had no windows and the door was shut. There was nowhere for the smoke to go. I heard a cough and a splutter. At that moment something pushed up against my back. The surprise knocked me forward. I tried to pull my hands apart but the rope cut deeper. The something was a someone. It was the girl from the circle. "Hi," she whispered.

She leant her head back upon my shoulder. Her long hair was so smoky that it made me cough.

"Ssshhh," she hissed, digging me in the ribs

with her elbow. "We don't want them to know we're awake."

But it was too late. I opened my eyes just long enough to see two huge shapes moving through the smoke, holding torches. I closed my eyes again and pretended to sleep. A huge, hairy hand squeezed my jaw and my eyes popped open. The man staring at me had a face black with soot and his hands were red with blood and blisters. As he snarled at me I could see that the few teeth he had were as black as his face.

"He wants to know how you want your eggs cooked," said the girl. She laughed. I didn't.

"What did he really say?"

"You don't want to know," she muttered.

The second man, who was slightly smaller but just as unfriendly, pulled us to our feet. He coughed and coughed again. Little bits of his breakfast fell on my face. When he grinned, I could see hunks of meat between his crooked teeth. I heard a rattling sound behind me. Smoke drifted towards the soft light of an open door. The fire began to spit sparks up towards the thatched roof. The two men ran to the fire, shouting at each other. One tripped over a bucket and screamed as he fell close to the fire. The girl chuckled and began to bounce towards the door. I bounced after her.

The chief stood at the door, blocking our exit with his mace. He shouted at the two men and they ran to their master like dogs. The girl laughed again. The house sizzled with grey smoke. They had drowned the fire with water.

The chief's men pushed us outside. The sun was hiding behind thick, dark clouds. I prayed that it would come out soon and save us. Many people stood outside their roundhouses. Some were looking up but most were looking at us. The chief looked at the sky and then to the men. Those watching cheered the words he shouted. A woman carrying a large bundle walked up to us. She gave the bundle to the men. They opened it, pulled out a linen gown and began to put in on the girl.

"Don't you have anything in blue – white's not my colour," she said. "And be careful with that fastening pin." She smiled when they began to dress me. I couldn't find anything to smile about.

A group of men, each wearing robes like ours, dragged a huge wooden sledge towards us.

"At least we won't have to walk," the girl said.

She was right. We were strapped to the sledge with leather cords. I lay there on my back, my head beside the girl's, looking up and praying for the sun to come out.

The people left their houses and began to walk beside us. They couldn't stop staring. Four women, each with chains of flowers around their necks, carried small pots. When they shook them, smoke blew over us. The smoke and the wobbling, wooden sledge made me feel dizzy.

A group of men had the job of placing wooden poles beneath the sledge. As we rolled over them, the men picked up the rollers from the back and then ran to the front to place them down again.

"Take your time," the girl said. "We're not in a hurry."

After that, the ride became even bumpier. The girl wasn't making things any better. We were rolling towards the stone circle.

A flock of ravens flew above us. They moved at the same speed as us as if they were part of the procession. More and more people joined us. Some walked along the high banks to get a good view. Many were chanting or singing. I saw the little girl who had been saved from the arrows. She wasn't chanting or singing.

"We've only been here one day," said the girl lying beside me. "How can it be our fault that the sun hasn't shone for weeks?"

"Is that what they're singing?" I asked.

She nodded. "They're going to burn the clouds away so the sun can come out."

"How are they going to do that?" I said.

I didn't have to wait long to find out. Standing in the circle, beside a huge, fallen stone, was the last person I wanted to see. Ecron was dressed in a bloodstained cloth and was holding a long, bronze dagger. A mighty fire was blazing and crackling behind her.

"They're going to burn us. That's the quickest way to reach the gods," the girl explained. "But don't worry – it won't hurt."

"Won't hurt?" I shouted.

"That's right – we'll already be dead."

The ravens flew away and sat upon the flat stones that topped the upright ones. They looked like huge stone door frames.

The sledge stopped when it reached the circle. The men raised the sledge so we could stand.

They cut the leather straps around us and tipped the sledge forward. We fell at Ecron's filthy feet. The chief's two 'dogs' lifted us up. Ecron began chanting. Her mask shook and the bones on her chest rattled. She chanted louder and louder as she held her arms up to the sky.

"Now would be a good time for the sun to come out," the girl said. The chief glared at her. The sun didn't come out. The bloodthirsty crowd cheered. The chief's men pushed us down and tied us to the stone altar. Ecron began chanting again and this time the crowd joined in. The four women placed their flowers around the stone and then began to swing their pots above us.

"I love that smell," the girl said.

The chanting was deafening. I thought it would be the last thing I'd ever hear. Ecron lifted the dagger high above her head and held it there. The chanting got even louder. Then Ecron threw her arms up into sky again and the crowd whispered and mumbled.

Ecron began to spin around faster and faster. She became a red blur. Then her blood red gown fell to the ground. Sunlight sparkled of her bronze chest plate. Ecron's arms pointed to the sky as she raised the dagger high above my head. I was going to die. The dagger plunged towards me. I shut my eyes and screamed, waiting for the pain... but the pain never came. When I opened my eyes, the bronze dagger was hanging in the air. It was glowing. The crowd fell silent as the animal mask and antlers fell to the ground. Whispered words buzzed around the circle. A face turned to look at us but it wasn't Ecron. It wasn't even a woman's face. It was the clean, smiling face of a tall man. He pointed his dagger towards the sky and shouted to the crowd. They all fell to the ground and held hands with the people next to them. Light burst into the circle. The stones shone bright white like giant teeth.

The chief gripped his mace tightly as he looked up at the man who had taken Ecron's place. I thought he was going to attack him; there was hate written on his face.

The man with the dagger knelt down and cut us free. "Let's get you out of here," he whispered.

Chapter 3

As we followed the man away from the circle, every part of my body hurt. My back ached and there were cuts all over my hands and feet.

"Those sledges were meant to pull stones, not children," the man said quietly.

The crowds were walking home. They seemed happy. Some of them were singing.

"It's amazing what difference a bit of sun makes," the man said, turning back to us. "Come on – keep up!"

There were so many things I wanted to ask him but I couldn't keep up with him. The girl limped beside me. "Lovely day for a walk, isn't it?" she said.

The man led us down to the banks of the river. "I think you could do with a rest – don't you?" We both nodded.

"And a wash," the girl added, her feet already in the water. She began to rub the soot and dirt from her face. "You need a wash more than me," she said, flicking water at me.

"We don't have time for that," the man said. He untied a long boat from a wooden platform and pulled it over to us. The boat was a kind of canoe made out of a large tree-trunk with its insides cut out. The girl got in first and then she held out her hand to help me in. Just as I went to grab it she took it away. I fell into the canoe. The girl laughed. The boat rocked as the man took his place at the back of the boat. He produced a paddle, dipped it into the water and we began to glide off downstream.

The rocking boat lulled me to sleep.

"Wake up sleepy head," the girl said, as she shook my shoulders. "You fell asleep to get out of paddling."

We got out of the boat and followed the man towards a small village. We walked across a bridge that arched over a wide, deep ditch. Slowly, it dawned on me that this was the village of roundhouses where I'd been held captive. I hadn't seen much of the village at the time. I was too worried about being sacrificed. The smell was the first thing I noticed. It was awful. I waved my hands in front of my nose.

"You get used to it after a bit," the man said. "I don't know why they keep these filthy pigs and cows so close to their houses."

The cows began to moo and the pigs snorted. The girl laughed.

"You've hurt their feelings," she said. She went up to their fenced pen and began to stroke the cows. "There, there," she said, "you're not *that* smelly."

There were plenty of animals but no people. They had all left their roundhouses to watch us die.

As we walked through the village we passed empty houses with crop fields behind them encircled by woven, wooden fences. There didn't seem to be much growing in the fields. There were small patches of ash outside some of the houses. Thin wisps of smoke blew from them. Half-eaten hunks of bread and meat lay on sheets of cloth.

"Looks like you disturbed their breakfast," chuckled the man. "They'll be back soon. We'd better hurry."

The man led us down a small winding path. At last, we reached the end of the village. The house at the end of it had a thatched roof with grass on top. Its walls were muddy white but close up I could see that this house was grander than all the others. It had a huge ditch around it and it wasn't round – it was rectangular.

Inside there was just enough light to see the wooden walls which split the house into six rooms. Animal skins hung on every wall.

Suddenly, a beam of light lit up the room. Our rescuer walked across the wooden floorboards and sat down on a beautifully carved pine chair, placing his bronze chest plate beside him. His necklace jangled. I stared at the different stones and beads on it – animal teeth, shells and small fossils. Golden beads and amber stones twinkled in the light. We sat on the floor opposite him, with our backs to the window.

"Nice house," the girl said.

"Thank you," replied the man, looking around.

All of a sudden the wooden wall behind the man began to move and a figure limped towards us. It was the tall boy from the stone circle.

"I believe you have met Rindef," the man said. We both nodded.

"You have him to thank for helping me to save you."

Rindef smiled at us. I smiled back. The girl said something and the boy smiled again.

"Rindef said he found you in the stone circle," the man said.

"Yes," I replied. "But I don't know how I got there. I can't remember anything before that day."

"Take your gowns off," ordered the man. We looked at each other and then did as he asked. We were both wearing long woollen shirts that hung over our knees. The end of a skirt poked out under our shirts, nearly reaching our brown sandals. We were both dressed like Rindef but with one difference. Our clothes looked brand new.

"Excuse my bad manners," the man said. "I'm a terrible host. I haven't even offered you a drink."

He spoke to Rindef. The boy disappeared behind a wooden wall. He returned carrying a large jug and three cups. He handed me a cup. It was a small, clay beaker with a round bottom and grooves cut into it. The boy poured the water.

"Drink up," said the man. "I have the best water in the village."

The water was disgusting. I wanted to spit it out but gulped it down instead. If he had the best water, I didn't want to drink anyone else's.

The man looked at me and laughed. His white teeth rattled. "I almost forgot about my other guest."

He got up and pulled back a wooden wall. An old woman was sat in the corner. She had cloth in her mouth and rope around her hands and feet.

"Ecron doesn't look quite so scary now?" said the man.

"She's even uglier without the mask," the girl said. Ecron glared at us. She shook her hands and feet but the ropes didn't move. She struggled like a wild beast in a trap.

"So you kidnapped her and took her place at the ceremony to rescue us?" I asked.

The man nodded.

"It was the only way to save you," he explained. "It was a bit of a long wait, but I knew the sun would come out at last."

"What will you do with Ecron now?" I asked.

"I'm finished with her. She is no use to me now," said the man. Rindef handed him a bronze dagger. The man walked up to Ecron. She shuffled back into the corner and scrunched herself up into a ball. She was shaking. Now she looked more like a trapped rabbit than a wild beast. I turned away. I couldn't watch him kill her.

He didn't. He only cut her ropes. She ran from the house screaming and waving her arms.

"Charming," the man said. "I don't think she enjoyed her stay."

"Aren't you worried she'll come back?" the girl asked. "She didn't look very pleased."

"She might bring the chief back," I agreed.

"You don't need to worry about the chief. You have nothing to fear," the man replied. He looked at Rindef. "Now, who'd like some more water?"

"Great," muttered the girl.

We sat down opposite the man again. Rindef gave us a bowl of raspberries. They tasted much better than the water.

"Let's return to what happened at the stone circle," said the man. "Don't you two recognise each other?"

We both shook our heads.

"No," I replied.

"Really?" he said.

The girl stared at me and then peered at her reflection in the shiny bronze breastplate. She stood up and put her head in her hands.

"Oh no, I don't believe it..." she said. She looked at me, and then turned to the man. "He's my twin brother, isn't he?"

The man smiled. I looked into the chest plate. My dirty face scowled back at me. Then I stared at the girl.

"You do look a bit like me but you're not as good looking," she said. "Your eyes are closer together, like a rat's. Your teeth are crooked and your head is too big for your body."

The man laughed. "You're definitely brother and sister."

If this really was my sister, it was news to me. I knew nothing about her. But I knew nothing about myself either.

"I can't remember anything before yesterday," I sighed.

I looked at the man for answers.

"It will come back to you – in time," he said. "Rindef for one was very pleased when you appeared in that circle. You saved his little sister."

For a moment, I stopped worrying about myself.

"Who were those warriors firing arrows at us? Why did they want to kill us?" I asked.

The man leant forward in his chair.

"Two tribes live in this land..." he began. "My people – the Lowlanders – and the Beakers who attacked you. Every year, at Midwinter, the two tribes used to feast together. The priestess would raise the Bronze Sun – a sacred relic used in the ceremony. When the Bronze Sun is raised, the real sun is pleased and it rises in the sky again."

"So what happened?" I asked him. "Why all the fighting?"

"The Bronze Sun is like a big coin that's split into three wedges. The Beakers think we Lowlanders stole a part of it because one of the wedges was taken from their chief's house."

"That's why they're so angry?" I asked.

"It's worse than that," said the man.

"The Lowlanders think that the Beakers stole OUR part of the Bronze Sun. That's disappeared too. They have declared war on us. We've declared war on them. Neither side will rest until they have their relic back.'

The man stood up and walked to the window. He seemed to be looking for something. Or someone.

"The sun has hardly shone since the day their

wedge was taken," he said. "Our priestess Ecron thought that you were Beaker children. With your big round heads and white teeth, you look just like them. That's why she wanted to sacrifice you to make the sun shine again."

My sister stood up.

"You're right about the white teeth but I don't have a big round head. He does though," she said, pointing at me.

The man laughed.

"You do. You both have big round Beaker heads. But that's good," he said.

"Good?" my sister and I said together.

"Yes," he said, "it will help you steal their bronze wedge.

My sister was as shocked as me to hear this. "We don't need to steal the wedge," she said, pointing outside. "The sun is shining without it."

The man smiled.

"You and your brother need the bronze wedge more than anyone else in this village," he said. "You need it to get home."

Chapter 4

I didn't get much sleep. The wooden mattress was hard and the animal skins weren't thick enough to keep me warm. I listened to the animals outside. There must have also been an animal inside; I could hear a soft scratching noise in the darkness.

At last, the sunlight poked through the thatched roof. When I pulled the wall of animal skins back I saw that my sister was asleep in the next room. I stepped over her and pulled the door open. It creaked but didn't wake her. There was a small fire burning in the fire pit. Wisps of smoke were drifting and dropping. I warmed my hands above the fire. The birds were up too, singing their morning song.

"You're up early," said a voice behind me. The man was carrying a large, round loaf of bread. "Did you sleep well?"

"Yes," I lied. The bed was almost as uncomfortable as the sledge.

He tore off a hunk of bread and threw it to me.

"My friend makes the best bread in the village," he said. The first bite wasn't too bad. "You can hardly taste the grit," he added.

I stopped eating. "The trick is not to bite too hard. If you do, you might end up losing a tooth!" said the man. I carried on eating, this time taking much smaller bites.

"Do you want some water to wash it down?" he asked. I didn't answer. I was chewing on a hard bit of bread. I just smiled and nodded.

"I'll make us some hot drinks," he said. He disappeared for a moment behind a wooden wall and returned with a copper kettle, covered in black scorch marks. He hung the kettle on a pole above the fire. Soon it was whistling.

"No one has one like this," he said. "I made it myself."

He looked very pleased with himself. It didn't look that special. He gave me a cup and sat down beside me.

The tea tasted better than I thought it would. It was very sweet. The man put down his cup: "It's flavoured with honey and the Meadowsweet herb. That's something else we learned from the

Beaker people."

The man looked up.

"Rain's coming," he said. Thin, white clouds were swaying in the sky, like a line of horses' tails.

"Really?" I said. "It looks like a nice day to me."

The man took a deep breath and sniffed a long sniff. I did the same.

"Did you smell the flowers?" he asked. "They smell so beautiful before the rain comes. And look at the smoke."

I did. It was just smoke.

"See how the smoke spirals up and then drops? That's because of the low pressure. And low pressure means rain. The moon last night was so sharp. Another sign that rain is coming."

"Amazing, "I said.

"Not really," he replied. "The villagers call me the 'Foreseer' because I tell them what weather is coming. They think I'm some kind of mystic. A shaman. Some even think I'm a god. But it's just science – mostly. I just look at things a little longer, that's all. Take the birds for example – they're flying low aren't they?"

I looked up. He was right.

"They always fly low when the rain is coming.

And your sister's hair. Take a look at it when she wakes up."

"I will," I said. I then thought about yesterday. "So you knew the sun was going to come out yesterday. You knew it would save us?" I asked him.

He nodded. "I hoped it would."

"What would have happened if the sun hadn't come out?" I asked.

He didn't answer. He stood and picked up the kettle.

"More tea I think," he muttered to himself.

The door creaked open behind me. My sister held her hands to her face to block out the sunlight. Her hair was curling up and going frizzy. She looked like she had a huge black spider sitting on her head. I started to laugh.

"What's so funny?" she said, angrily.

"Nothing," I said. "The Foreseer has just told me a joke. That's all."

"Oh, right," she said. "The Foreseer?"

The Foreseer nodded.

"Sit down and have some bread. It's really tasty," I told my sister.

I gave her a huge chunk. "The trick is to take

big hard bites," I said.

After breakfast, the Foreseer took us back into his house. He sat down on his chair.

"You two will steal back the bronze wedge from the Beakers tonight," he said. "You will walk into their village. If they see you they will think that you are Beaker children."

"Thanks," spluttered the girl. My sister seemed to have some bread stuck in her throat. She coughed and then spoke again.

"Do they speak the same language as your tribe. Will I understand them?"

"Not at first," the Foreseer replied. "But you soon will, just as quickly as you began to understand Ecron and the chief, Therorb."

He was right. At first, my sister had no idea what the people were saying but she soon began to. I only understood a few of their words.

"You'll need Beaker names," he said.

He began to scratch letters into the chalk. A-U-R-O-C-H. He looked up at me. "You're a strong looking boy. You look like a Auroch."

"A what?" I asked.

"Auroch are wild cattle," he said. "With big horns."

"And bad breath," added my sister. "Perfect."

I wasn't happy and the Foreseer could tell. He scratched out some of the chalk signs and wrote the word H-A-R-O-C-U.

"If you don't like the sound of Auroch, how about Harocu instead?" he asked.

The anagram had a solid ring to it.

He wrote another word into the chalk.

N-E-V-I-X. He looked at my sister. "Rindef says that you are a fast runner. And I think you're quite cunning too. Nevix is perfect."

She smiled weakly.

"It's better than Vixen I suppose," she added.

We planned the robbery together. The Foreseer was going to take us to the edge of the Beaker village. Then we would have to get past the two men who guarded the bronze wedge in the Great Hall.

The Foreseer handed us a small animal skin pouch. "It's a sleeping herb called henbane," he explained. "Put a few leaves and seeds at the bottom of their cups; they'll be snoring in no time."

The Foreseer made it sound so easy – drug the guards, steal the bronze wedge and run back here.

"Anything else?" I asked.

"One last thing," he added. "It's really important. Do not touch the wedge with your bare hands."

"If we get the wedge back for you, can you help to get us home?" I asked.

He never answered. He just handed us each a pair of leather gloves.

It was almost dark when we left the Foreseer's home. Thick, grey clouds hung low in the sky. "Rain is coming," he said.

"How do you know? Is it because the birds have stopped singing?" I asked.

"No, I just felt a drop on my head," he said.

We walked for miles, keeping to the low ground on a path through the woods. "It's not the quickest way but it is the safest," the Foreseer told us.

The trees were so close together that there was no light in the woods. Thick clouds hid the moon. Raindrops dripped from the branches. I followed the sounds of the Foreseer's footsteps. I could hear my sister following close behind.

We stopped near the edge of the woods. The

Foreseer pointed with his mace.

"Their village is on the other side of the woods," he said.

He handed my sister a small pouch and two cups. "Time for me to leave," he whispered.

He gave me a small, copper knife. I tucked it under my tunic. "Nevix and Harocu – you know what to do. And don't forget to wear the gloves."

I nodded, too frightened to think straight.

"Come on," urged Nevix. "We've got work to do."

The Foreseer disappeared into the gloom. We were alone. I wrapped my cloak around me to keep the rain out. We moved through the trees on the very edge of the woods until the village was right in front of us. The round houses were glowing like ovens. We couldn't see any people. We moved out of the woods and walked into the village, staying away from the houses.

"This way," said Nevix. I followed her. I could see her in the dim light from the houses.

We'd been told to make for the Great Hall, where the bronze wedge was kept. It was a big rectangular building in the heart of the Beaker's village. As we edged closer to the stone buildings,

I stumbled, lost balance and found myself sliding down a steep grass ditch. I dug my heels into the wet slope to stop myself falling. Suddenly, a hand grabbed my wrist. My sister had me by the cloak, gritting her teeth as she tried to pull me back up the slope. I pushed up with my feet and slowly, I clambered out of the ditch.

"The Foreseer didn't forsee this ditch," said Nevix, letting go of my ripped cloak.

"Neither did I," I said, fighting for breath. "What are we going to do?"

"The only thing we can do," replied my sister. "We're going to jump it."

My sister said she'd go first. I didn't argue and stood watching as she took a few steps back and then sprinted. Nevix flung herself forward and landed on the other side of the ditch. She rolled into a ball and then stood up and waved.

She'd made it look easy. I took a deep breath and ran towards the ditch. I stopped before I reached it. The moon now peaked out from behind the clouds. I could see my sister's worried face.

I told myself I could do it. I imagined myself flying over the ditch. I took an even bigger breath and ran. I jumped, earlier than I should. I looked down and then wished I hadn't. A cruel line of sharpened wooden spears were pointing up at me. I began to panic as I fell. I wasn't going to make it but my sister reached out to grab me. My hands touched her arms but slid back to her wrists. I was slipping but she yanked so hard that I fell forward and landed on top of her.

"Get off," she hissed.

"Thanks," I puffed. I was shaking all over. "Now what?"

"We can't just walk in," my sister said.

She was right. The wooden bridge that stood at the entrance to the great hall had been raised. It blocked the small door. There was no way in. We could see inside through the gaps in the planks. Torches flickered in each corner of the hall. A huge wooden table stretched from the door to the wall. Two guards sat at the end of the table. They were eating and drinking. I looked above them and gasped. The bronze wedge seemed to be floating in the air. It was inside a golden case.

Chapter 5

We made a plan. I began to whistle. We waited. Nothing happened. I whistled again, louder this time. Nothing happened. I picked up some stones and threw them against the bridge. The bridge rattled, louder than I expected. At last we heard voices and scraping chairs followed by the sound of footsteps. The bridge creaked and groaned as it began to drop. Then I ran to my hiding place.

I heard two men walk over the bridge. Their voices got louder as they moved closer. I took a deep breath and held on tight. Their voices began to fade as they moved away. I heard them walk back over the bridge and into the great hall. I waited.

I heard the bridge being raised again. Now all I could hear was the patter of rain and the sound of feet stepping lightly over the bridge.

Suddenly I began to move. Someone was pulling the rope. I clung tightly to it as I looked up. There was a figure at the top of the well where I was hiding.

"It's alright," my sister whispered. "It worked."

I nearly fell out of the bucket as it bumped against the sides of the well.

We stood on the bridge and looked into the great hall. Both guards were slumped on the table and they were breathing deeply. The henbane herbs had worked. I followed my sister inside. She jumped up onto the table.

"Get up on here," she whispered. "I can't do it on my own."

I held out my hand and she pulled me up with her gloved hand. We walked to the end of the table and stepped over the sleeping guards. The bronze wedge was swaying above us, tied to a rafter.

"Kneel down," my sister ordered. She climbed onto my shoulders. I stood up. She reached out to grab the wedge but couldn't reach it.

"Maybe if I stand on your shoulders..." she whispered. I held her feet. She wobbled as she reached up. Stretching up she managed to touch the golden case but couldn't grip it. I lowered her down onto the table.

"Now what?" I asked. My sister was looking at the guards. "You have got to be joking!" I said.

We managed to get the smaller man off his chair without waking him. The henbane was still working. We lifted his heavy wooden chair onto the table. I stood on the chair. My sister stood on my shoulders. We wobbled. The chair creaked. The man on the floor began to stir.

"Hurry up!" I said.

She touched the case of the relic but she couldn't quite get hold of it. It swayed on the rope. She had to wait for the case to swing back to her. This time she grabbed the rope and pulled down on it. It didn't move. The wooden rafter groaned. So did the guard on the floor. He was beginning to wake up.

"The knife," she said.

I held her leg with one hand and reached beneath my tunic with the other. I felt for the knife. The guard yawned. I handed the knife to my sister. She began to cut.

"This knife is rubbish," she said. "It'll take ages!"

"We haven't got ages," I told her.

The guard stretched his arms as my sister sawed at the rope. I looked at the guard. He was now looking at me. He stood up and staggered back against the wall. He then steadied himself, pulled out his dagger and stumbled towards us.

"Got it!" shouted my sister. The guard was on the table. I looked down at him. He thrust his knife at me. My brave sister jumped off my shoulders and kicked it from his hand. Her next kick took the guard in the stomach and sent him crashing to the floor. She had knocked him out.

We ran along the table and I picked up a torch. I could hear the man on the chair stirring. We dashed across the bridge, leapt over the ditch and ran out into the night. I heard shouting behind me. I turned and threw the torch onto the wooden bridge. But the bridge was too wet to burn. A guard stood at the door. He was screaming at us. Soon the whole village would be awake.

I ran after my sister. She was disappearing into the woods and I couldn't keep up with her. As we ran we heard lots of shouting coming from the village.

"Come on, keep up!" cried my sister as she moved through the darkness. The moonlight cut through the branches and shone on the golden case in her hand. The village was beginning to light up. Flaming torches were moving towards the woods. The Beakers were coming.

We ran deeper into the woods. Branches cut my hands and scraped my face. The noise behind us was louder now. Men were shouting and dogs were barking.

We kept running. My legs burnt as I tried to keep up with my sister. I heard horses. They were riding around the edge of the woods. I stopped. I could hardly breathe. We looked back and saw a line of flames moving through the trees towards us. We ran into the darkness like hunted animals. There was no time to stop and think. We both knew what would happen if we were caught.

I saw my sister fall. She had tripped over a tree root and lay groaning on the ground. The bronze wedge had fallen from the case and lay against a tree. I went to pick it up…

My body shook. Images flashed. Many faces, most of them smiling. A room. A huge white room span. A golden flash. A scream.

My sister was shaking me. I was lying on the floor. I was so cold yet sweat was dripping off me.

"Stop screaming!" she said. "They'll find us."

"What happened?" I asked.

"You picked up the wedge – without gloves on," she said. "You should have picked me up instead!"

She smiled but not for long. The flames were so close we could feel their heat. We could see the figures holding them. A hand came through the trees and pulled my sister into the woods. My sister vanished in front of me. A tall, hooded figure stood over me and lifted me to my feet.

"Quick," he said. "Follow me."

It was Rindef. He opened a small wooden hatch that was hidden in the muddy ground. I looked down and saw my sister's smiling face looking up at me.

"Get in," she called.

I jumped into the hole and Rindef lowered himself down after me, closing the hatch behind him. We sat huddled together in complete darkness. The villagers were now very close. They were right above us. We didn't talk. I tried to stop breathing. I could hear their dogs sniffing at the ground. They could smell us.

Chapter 6

"Wake up. Wake up. We need to go." I was woken by Rindef's hand shaking me and my sister's voice calling. The dogs and Beakers had gone. The only sound was the birds singing. Slowly, Rindef opened the hatch. Soft light crept into the hole. It was almost morning.

We followed Rindef through the woods. He limped but he limped quickly. My sister was limping too. He slowed down when we reached the edge of the woods. I recognised where we were. The winding river stretched away from us, towards the village.

"Rindef uses that hiding hole when he spies on the Beaker People," my sister explained. "His father is one of the most important men in the village. He works for him, collecting information. The Foreseer told him to stay there, just in case we ran into trouble."

"I'm glad he did," I said.

The Foreseer was outside his home, sat in

front of a fire. He looked pleased to see us. He looked even happier when my sister showed him the bronze wedge.

When we were inside the Foreseer took the relic and looked at it closely. He turned it upside down and traced the markings with his finger.

"Well done," he said. "I told you it would be easy."

"Easy?" my sister began. "I can hardly walk!"

The Foreseer laughed: "There's always a flip side," he said, turning the wedge over.

I slept for hours. When I woke, the sun was low in the sky. Steam was rising behind the house. I found the Foreseer stood beside a long trough of boiling water. He was holding a pair of tongs in the fire. When he pulled them out, I saw a white-hot arrowhead on the end. The water hissed and fizzed when he dropped the arrowhead in.

"Boiled ham for tea," he said. "You must be starving." He was right.

The ham tasted good. I was eating my third chunk when we saw Rindef limping down the lane. He was moving quickly and had a look of panic on his face. He spoke to the Foreseer.

"What are we going to do?" my sister asked.

"We're going to meet them," said the Foreseer.

The village was full of people. Women were picking up children, taking them inside their houses. Men were walking past, carrying bows and arrows or bronze axes. We walked with the men. Some were strapping on wrist guards and others were swinging their axes. We followed them to the edge of the village. Therorb, the village leader was on horseback and our old friend Ecron stood beside him. She snarled at us. The Foreseer blew her a kiss. The men lined up in rows behind their leader. Rindef joined them.

We stood close to the Foreseer to the side of the warriors. Many of them were staring at us. They stopped looking at us when a small group of riders approached.

"It's Zerban, the leader of the Beaker people," the Foreseer whispered. We knew why he was here.

Therorb rode out to meet him with two riders on either side. When the two chiefs were face to face the shouting began. Zerban shouted at Therorb. Therorb shouted back. I couldn't understand the words but I knew what they were arguing about. I was shaking. I was terrified that one of the Beakers would recognise me.

The ground began to move. My feet trembled. A long shape appeared in the distance. It looked blurry beneath the sun. As it came closer, it became clearer. It was an army. There were hundreds of men, mostly on horseback.

Our warriors got ready. The archers strung their first arrows. The men with axes gripped them tighter.

"There has been too much killing," the Foreseer said. He smiled at us both and then walked out to join the two chiefs. The shouting began again but soon turned to talking. I was amazed when the archers lowered their bows and the axe men put down their weapons.

The two chiefs turned and rode back to their armies. The Foreseer walked back towards us.

"There will be no fighting, at least, not today," he told us.

"How did you manage that?" I asked.

"I appealed to Zerban's better nature. We struck a bargain. There won't be a fight. There will be a contest."

"What sort of contest?" my sister asked.

"A race," he said. "A race between two people:

one from each village. The winning village wins both bronze wedges."

"Wow. No pressure then. I wouldn't want to be our runner," I said. "Who do you think will be chosen?"

The Foreseer turned to my sister.

"How bad is your leg?" he asked her.

We walked back through the village. Women and children stood outside their houses. They were smiling at my twin sister. She smiled and waved back at them.

"Walk. Don't limp," the Foreseer said to her.

The Foreseer told us more when we were back inside his home. "We have three days," he began. "In three days Nevix must race the Beaker's champion. She will circle the stones three times," he said.

"Three days?" I said.

The Foreseer stood still and looked down at us.

"Yes. Three days. Zerban wanted to race there and then. He doesn't trust us but I bought us some time."

"Three days," Nevix said. "I can hardly walk. I won't be able to run in three days' time."

"You will," the Foreseer said. His face was firm. "I have something to treat your leg with. It will be fine by then."

"What will happen if she can't run?" I asked. The Foreseer turned away and spoke with his back to us.

"Then we lose," he said. "No one else in the village can beat their champion Raktes. They will come again and I won't be able to stop them."

Rindef walked into the house. He put his axe down and sat with us.

"Raktes," he said, shaking his head. He said some other words. My sister understood them.

"Bigger, stronger and faster than a horse!" she said. "How can I beat him?"

"By running faster than him," the Foreseer said. "Raktes is the chief's eldest son. They call him the stag."

"Great," mumbled my sister. "A huge stag against a tiny fox. There can only be one winner."

The Foreseer turned around. He looked and sounded angry. "Yes… you. You will win. You have to. You'll win and you will save many lives."

My sister stood up to face him. "And if I lose," she said, "What will happen to me?"

The Foreseer looked at her but didn't speak. He looked at Rindef. Finally, he turned back to Nevix. "You won't lose," he said.

My sister spent most of the next day resting. She lay on her back with her injured leg raised. The Foreseer rubbed on the herbs and flowers that Rindef and I had collected.

"More berries," she ordered. She smiled as I brought them over. "I could get used to being fed by a slave," she said.

"Raktes will be eating raw meat for breakfast," I said.

She stopped smiling. "Go away, I need some sleep," she moaned.

Many villagers gathered outside the house. They wanted to see their champion training and find out just how fast Nevix could run. They shouted her name but our new 'champion' stayed inside. The crowd began to shuffle back to the village. They left muttering and shaking their heads.

I spent the days before the race with Rindef. We picked more fruit for Nevix. We cooked meats and collected water for her. We searched the woods for herbs and spices. Rindef even washed her linen cloak. She didn't thank us once. She just grinned each time I brought her something and then laughed with the Foreseer. They always stopped talking when they saw me. I began to feel jealous. I wasn't even sure I wanted her to win.

Chapter 7

When the day of the race arrived, a small group of people gathered outside, cheering for Nevix. They looked nervous, even scared. Mothers hugged their children tight and whispered into their ears. The Foreseer stood gazing at the sky. The sun was huge and it only had a few thin clouds for company. The palest of white moons blurred beside it.

"A beautiful day for a race," he said. Nevix smiled at him. Her white gown glowed and her necklace of coloured stones sparkled in the sunlight. A small girl ran from the crowd and placed a ring of bright flowers around her neck.

The crowds got thicker as we approached the stone circle. They lined the avenue as before but this time they were cheering instead of jeering. Black ravens sat upon shining white stones. The tallest stones were strewn with flowers.

Young children ran in front of us and dropped flowers. Nevix waved at the crowds as they cheered her name. Our chief Therorb stood by a flat stone at the circle's entrance. His necklaces and bones rattled as he waved his mace in the air and shouted my sister's name. The crowd took up the chant.

The deep ditch around the stones sparkled like a silver ring. Men had worked night and day to dig it deeper and wider to make the white chalk shine again. The villagers stood along the edges on the far side. A long, loud horn blast came from the avenue. The Beaker people were coming. Two men on horseback rode towards us with a horde of people walking behind them. We could hear their shouts and songs before we could see them.

The two men on horseback climbed down from their horses. One was their chief, Zerban. The other was taller than any man I had ever seen before. He stood in front of a stone and almost blocked it. I wondered how my sister could beat such a beast.

His people gathered around the far side of the ditch. They stamped their feet and chanted for Raktes. When he ripped off his cloak, they stamped and chanted even louder. His body looked as hard as stone. He had muscles on his muscles. His bronzed body glowed beneath the midday sun. He strutted around in front of his cheering crowd. His nickname, Stag, was a good one.

The Foreseer held out a thick rope. My sister removed her necklace and her garlands of flowers then grabbed the rope and climbed slowly down into the deep ditch. She looked tiny and scared, more like a mouse than a vixen. Raktes jumped into the ditch. A cloud of chalk turned Nevix's hair white. She stood facing her opponent.

The people around the ditch moved closer. Mothers pulled their children back to stop them falling in. Therorb stuck his mace into the ground. Its shining blue head marked the finish line.

Therorb lifted a huge horn. The crowds cheered for their champions and stamped their feet, kicking dust into the air. I looked down at my sister. She stood shoulder to waist with the Beaker giant.

A blast from the horn started the race and a huge cheer followed. Raktes knocked Nevix to the ground with his elbow and raced off. The villagers groaned then cheered when she got to her feet and cheered even louder when she began to chase Raktes.

I could see the Beaker's head bobbing quickly around the circle. There was a huge chalk dust trail flowing behind him. My sister's trail was smaller but was getting closer. The crowds screamed when the runners passed them. Even the birds joined in, flapping their wings and squawking.

Raktes ran towards me. My sister was right behind him. She tried to run around him but he blocked her with his huge arms. Nevix was faster but she couldn't get past the wall of muscle. She tried again to run around his huge legs but he shoved her over. My sister lay coughing on the ground. Therorb blew his horn as Raktes ran past the mace. The Beaker people shouted and screamed wildly as their champion raced towards them. He slowed down and waved at them. He shouldn't have done that.

Nevix was up and running. Her dust trail was streaking around the circle. The shouts from the Beaker people warned Raktes that Nevix was close behind. I could see glimpses of her through the chalk cloud. Once again, she tried to run around the giant. He blocked her. She tried to pass him on the right side. He blocked her again. She dashed towards the left. He held out his hand again to stop her but she wasn't there. He couldn't see her but I could. She was running up the walls of the ditch. Before he could react, Nevix flipped through the air and landed in front of him. Our villagers screamed and jumped up and down. Therorb blew his horn again.

The thin trail of white smoke began to race away from Raktes. Nevix was running away from him. He couldn't catch her. She was going to win. I looked at the Foreseer. He looked horrified. I heard my sister scream.

The Beaker people were throwing stones down into the ditch. The chalk cloud was no longer moving. I ran through the stone circle to the other side. I got there just before Raktes. My sister was lying on the floor, blood pouring from the cuts on her arms and legs. Raktes ran towards her and kicked her in the leg. His people cheered with joy. Our people screamed with hate. Therorb blew the horn three times. Nevix had lost.

The Foreseer and I pulled my sister up from the ditch. Chalk covered her ripped gown and she had patches of blood on her arms and legs. She fell to the ground. Zerban walked up to us. Raktes was beside him. He smiled as he wiped the chalk from his body. A large group of Beaker men carrying bronze swords crossed the ditch and stood behind their chief. They gathered around Nevix and lifted her off the ground. She struggled but couldn't break free from their tight grip.

Our villagers were yelling at the Beaker people who shouted back from the far side of the stone circle. We stood in the middle with a ring of noise and hatred around us.

Zerban raised his mace. His people stopped shouting. Therorb did the same and our people fell silent too.

It was then I noticed the cold and darkness even though it was the middle of the day and the sun was shining.

The two chiefs walked into the centre of the circle and stood between two huge stones. They talked for a moment. Therorb nodded and returned to the circle. Zerban and his men began to drag my sister away. She screamed.

The Foreseer ran towards them but stopped when he got close to the sharp swords. He ran to Therorb and began to shout at the chief. Our people, still stood behind the ditch, were howling like dogs. Some were throwing stones at the Beaker warriors. Therorb waved his mace at them but they didn't stop yelling until their leader Zerban blew his horn.

The horn blast was a signal to a large group of Beaker warriors who had been hiding beyond the avenue. Now they were marching towards us. The Beaker warriors stopped and stood side by side: longbows at the front, axes and swords behind them.

The Foreseer looked to the sky then at Nevix. The stones' shadows stretched out across the circle. It was getting even darker and even colder. Zerban's men pulled Nevix towards the cheering Beaker people.

The Foreseer walked out in front of the Beakers. He spoke to them with his mace in the air. Zerban and his son looked to the sky then looked to each other. They laughed. The Foreseer began to shout at the Beaker chief. He pointed to my sister and then back to the sun. The chief laughed again and began to walk away. The people around the ditch gasped and pointed to the sky. They started muttering, repeating the same thing. It sounded like praying.

I looked at the sun. It was incredible. It looked like the gods had bitten a chunk from it. The moon's shadow was moving across it. It was getting even darker. Zerban and his son looked at each other. They were scared. The Foreseer spoke to them. When he stopped, they looked terrified.

A diamond ring of light around the moon was all that was left of the sun. It was almost pitch black and freezing cold. Day had turned to night. The Beaker people were screaming now. The two horses were neighing nervously. The men holding Nevix let go of her and ran to join their people. Nevix hobbled over to me. I hugged her tight. She was cold and shaking.

Zerban and Raktes tried to climb onto their frightened horses. They needed help steadying them. Once they were on, they galloped off into the darkness. The warriors turned and followed their chief back down the avenue. The Beaker people around the ditch joined them. The Beaker people were gone.

Slowly the sun began to re-emerge from behind the moon. Our people were still standing around the ditch. Some were crying. Others were still chanting. The Foreseer stood on the stone table to talk to them. There was no sign of Therorb. He had disappeared into the darkness. Sunlight shone on the Foreseer. Day had returned.

Rindef and I helped Nevix back to the village. I really wanted to know what the Foreseer had said to the people. I understood some words, like 'The Sun' and 'Stone Circle' but not much more. We helped my sister into her bed. Rindef and I went off to collect herbs and water. When we returned, she was asleep. The Foreseer was sitting on his chair beside her.

"What just happened?" I asked him. "What did you say? Why did the Beaker people leave? What's going to happen to the Bronze Sun now?"

The Foreseer leant forward in his chair and smiled. "I will tell you everything when your sister wakes up.

Chapter 8

We hadn't been home long when the first well-wishers came. When the Foreseer told them Nevix was asleep, they looked disappointed. They left behind all sorts of presents: fruits and berries, jugs of honeyed mead, decorated pots full of flowers, necklaces of rubies and stones, even a carved walking stick. I smiled. Only a few days ago these people wanted us dead. The Foreseer smiled too.

"You won't have to go fruit picking again," he said.

Nevix slept for the rest of the day. She didn't stir once. Not even when the Foreseer rubbed his foul smelling mixture into her cuts.

When I woke in the morning, I found Nevix outside. She was sat down, her back against a woven fence, poking the fire with her walking stick. She looked terrible and she didn't smell any better. Flies buzzed around the green paste that oozed from her cuts.

"How are you feeling?" I asked her. I couldn't think of anything better to say. She shook her head and sighed. She swatted a fly above her knees.

"Where are the Foreseer and Rindef?" I asked. She just shrugged her shoulders.

"Fancy some berries. We have enough to feed the whole village," I said. I laughed. My sister didn't. We sat in silence for ages. I threw bits of wood onto the fire to keep it burning.

At last, she spoke:

"Do you remember anything about where we're from? Anything about our parents – anything about our home. Anything at all?"

I shook my head. "No, I don't remember anything Nevix."

"Don't call me that," she said angrily. "That's not my name."

"Do you know what is?" I asked her.

She began to beat the fire with her stick. "No. But I'm sure I'm not named after some stupid animal."

"The Foreseer said that he will tell us everything," I said. She shook her head and turned to me.

"Do you trust him?" she asked. I hadn't thought about that until now.

"Don't you?" I said. She pushed herself up with the stick.

"There's something not quite right about him. He's different. He doesn't fit in around here," she said.

I chuckled. "Neither do we. He saved you. You have a lot to thank him for."

Just then I saw the Foreseer walking down the path towards us. Rindef was limping behind him. "You can thank him now."

"Good to see you up and about," called the Foreseer. "How are your cuts and bruises?"

"Smelly," Nevix said.

"Perfect – that means they're healing," the Foreseer replied. My sister didn't look convinced. She swatted the flies that were trying to eat her elbow.

"Where have you been?" I asked him.

"Rindef and I had to attend a meeting in the village," he said, looking at the boy. Rindef had a huge grin on his face. The Foreseer continued: "Therorb has disappeared. No-one knows where he is. The village elders have been electing a new chief."

"But what if he comes back?" I asked.

"He won't be back," Rindef said, coldly. "Not after what he did. He was going to give your sister to the Beakers."

The Foreseer nodded. He looked sad. "Rindef's right," he said. "He won't ever show his face around here – not if he's got any sense.

My sister used her new walking stick to help her hobble over to the Foreseer.

"So who is the new chief?" she asked.

Rindef's grin grew even wider.

"Veronus," he said. "My father. Isn't that great!"

Rindef turned and headed back towards the village. He looked so happy.

"This is good news for all of us," the Foreseer said. We both looked blankly at him.

"What do you mean?" I asked him.

He didn't answer. Instead, he walked into the house. We followed him in. My sister sat in his chair. I stood beside her, opposite the Foreseer.

"Veronus is weak," he said.

"And that's good for us?" I said, confused.

The Foreseer nodded. "It is. He will do what I tell him. I'm as good as the chief now."

My sister looked up from the floor. "But aren't you scared about Zerban? He will know that we have a weak chief. He might attack us again."

The Foreseer laughed softly.

"We don't need to worry about him. Not for a while at least. Not after what I said to him."

My sister and I spoke together: "What did you say to him?"

"I said that their cheating, at our most ancient monument, had dishonoured him and his people. I told him that he had angered the sun. I warned him the sun would take revenge."

I shook my head. I didn't understand what I was hearing. "So you knew that it was going to happen. You knew that the moon was going to cover the sun."

The Foreseer smiled. "I was confident," he said.

"How did you know? Was it the weather? Or the birds?" I asked him.

The Foreseer clapped his hands. "Well done – you're learning very quickly."

My sister was right. Something didn't make sense. I wasn't sure if I believed what he was saying.

"But you chose that day for the race," I told the Foreseer. "You chose the actual day when the sun disappeared."

The Foreseer didn't answer. He fumbled with his hands and then tapped his fingers together. "I can see why he chose you," he said to me. "There's something I need to show you."

He pushed back the woven fencing and walked into the room at the back of the house. We followed him in. He peeled a patch of leather off the wall. There were many chalk marks on the hard mud. I stared at the numbers at the bottom. Only one number had not been crossed out: 10,585. The Foreseer picked up a stick of chalk and crossed it out.

I looked at the very top of the muddy wall. More numbers had been written down: 21.6.1970.

"The day I arrived," the Foreseer explained.

On the wall, between the two numbers, were thousands of white lines. It was a tally count. The white lines got smaller and smaller as they went down the wall.

"I have scraped a mark every day since I arrived," the Foreseer said. My sister and I stared at each other. Our eyes and mouths were open wide.

"Arrived from where?" my sister asked.

"The same place as you," the Foreseer replied.

"What place?" Nevix said.

"You'd better sit down again," he told her.

My sister lowered herself into the chair. She was staring, wide-eyed at the Foreseer who put his hands together and began to tap his fingers. We waited for him to tell us more.

"A place far from here," he said. "I've been waiting for you. You just took a lot longer than I expected." He pointed to some chalk marks on the floor. He had a weak smile on his face.

My sister didn't seem to believe a word he said. "So where are we from? And why were we sent here?" she demanded.

The Foreseer walked towards Nevix. When he saw the anger on her face, he stopped.

"You've travelled a very long time to get here," he said. "And you were sent here for the same reason as me: to complete the Bronze Sun. Once you have all three wedges you can return home."

My sister sat shaking her head in disbelief.

"But we only have one piece," I said. "The one we stole from the Beaker people."

The Foreseer looked at me but didn't speak. A smile came back to his face.

"That's not completely true," he said. "Wait here."

He opened and closed a couple of woven fences to reach the end of the house. My sister and I stared at each other. She looked very pale. We heard wood creaking and groaning. The Foreseer returned, closing the fences on his way back to us. He held a wrapped parcel in his gloved hand. Slowly, he began to unwrap it. I knew what was in that parcel before he showed us.

"Two bronze wedges," Nevix said, now leaning forward. "Where did you get the second one from?"

"It's also from the Beaker village," the Foreseer said. "I stole it from Zerban's house."

He moved his gloved hand over the markings on both sides of one wedge.

"Where is the last piece?" I asked him. "Do the Beaker people have it?"

The Foreseer shook his head.

"So we have it?" my sister asked.

"Yes…and no," he explained. "The last piece is a long way from here. It's beyond our reach. We can't get it back."

My sister groaned and slumped back in the chair. "So, we're stuck here forever," she said, "with stony bread and dirty water."

"I didn't say that," the Foreseer said. "We have two thirds of the Bronze Sun – enough to make a third piece."

"What do you mean?" my sister said. She was sitting up again.

The Foreseer was grinning. "There is a smith in this land who may be able to cast a third wedge from the other two. He might be able to complete the patterns. You'll then be one step closer to going home."

"One step closer," I said. "What else do we have to do?"

The Foreseer began to walk away from us, towards the door. He turned back to talk to us. "That's enough information for now. I'll tell you more at the feast tonight."

He turned away from us and walked out of the door. The Foreseer had promised to tell us everything. He hadn't.

Chapter 9

Everyone wanted to look good for the feast. My sister wore gold beads in her silky hair and had a garland of flowers around her neck.

Nevix wasn't the only one wearing flowers. Most of the women and many of the girls wore them too. Anyone who had jewellery wore it. No-one looked better than our new chief Veronus. His pure gold breastplate and crescent shaped lunula pendant, which hung from his neck, shone beneath the full moon. Golden armlets wrapped his forearms and threads of gold glistened in his hair. Rindef walked behind his father. He was wearing his bright red tunic and a big smile.

Our new chief looked nervous, but our old friend Ecron didn't. She walked beside the chief, waving her stick, looking to the moon and muttering something under her breath. The crowd cheered and shouted the name of their chief. Children threw flowers at his feet and men beat their feet and spears against the ground.

They cheered even louder when Ecron presented the blue-headed mace to the new chief.

"They're cheering because they like the new chief," I said to the Foreseer. "Yes," he said. "But it's also because it means the feast can start."

It was a great feast. It seemed the people had been saving themselves for such an occasion. They roasted meat on spits and sizzled fish on hot stones. The people sang and danced when they weren't feasting. The Foreseer left us and spoke to the new chief for some time. When he walked back over to us, he had a smile on his face.

"He has agreed. You're as good as home now," he said.

Nevix and I both stared at him. We had no idea what he was talking about.

"The new chief has agreed to rebuild the stone circle. When the new circle stands complete, you will be able to return home."

For a moment, we didn't know what to say. "That's great," I said, finally. "How did you manage to convince him?"

"He didn't take much convincing," the Foreseer said. "I just told him that if he wanted to please the sun god and avoid another blackout, he should restore the stone circle to its former glory. I didn't mention you and the bronze wedges."

"So we're nearly home then," my sister said, looking up at the Foreseer.

He nodded.

"How long will it take to rebuild the stone circle?" I asked him.

"Sixty sunrises," he said.

We walked back to the roundhouse without the Foreseer. He said he had business with the new chief. I must have fallen asleep because I was woken by a creaking and groaning sound. A sudden fear gripped me when I heard the unfamiliar noises. Was there an intruder in the house?

I got up quietly and wrapped my furs tightly around my shoulders. I moved in the dark towards the noise. I edged slowly forward with one hand in front of me through the darknes. My hands trembled as I touched the animal skins on the walls and then found the Foreseer's long handled mace. I prayed I didn't have to use it.

The creaking sound had stopped. The only noises came from outside. An owl hooted and the leaves on the trees rustled in the night breeze.

Perhaps there was no one else there? Maybe I had dreamt it all?

I turned around and began to walk back to bed. A noise from behind stopped me. There *was* someone else in the house. I spun round to face the intruder but was immediately punched to the floor by a gloved hand. I fell back, crashing into pots and vases. I picked up the mace and swung it wildly but I didn't hit anything. The stone head of the mace scraped and screamed as it struck the wall. A blow took me in the face and forced me back. The intruder ran out of the house, knocking things over on the way. I pushed myself up and chased after the intruder.

The full moon lit the road towards the village. There was no one on the path so I ran around to the back of the house. A tall figure was disappearing into the woods. I sprinted to catch them up but trees blocked the moonlight.

The figure had disappeared into the darkness. I couldn't see a thing but I could hear heavy footsteps fading away ahead of me. Refusing to give up, I ran towards the sound.

Branches scraped my arms and legs. Twigs and stones cut into my bare feet but I kept chasing the footsteps. I was getting closer.

Then the footsteps were gone. I could still hear the breathing though. It was close, just ahead on the other side of a thick clump of trees. I stopped running and walked towards it. I wished I still had the mace. My heart was thumping and sweat trickled down my face. My nose was still bleeding from the blow to my face. I spat the blood from my mouth.

Suddenly I saw a glimpse of a figure moving in through the trees ahead. It was too dark to see its face. I strode forward with clenched fists, ready to fight. The figure caught sight of me and took off again, glancing back over its shoulder to look at me. Then the figure let out of cry of pain and dropped to the floor. It had run headfirst into a thick branch and been knocked to the ground.

The figure lay face down with the stolen object still in its hand. I picked up the wrapped parcel and walked out into the moonlight to examine the contents. I slipped my hand under the cloth.

My body shook. I was in the room again. Tall, white shapes were spinning. A man was staring at me. He had dark hair and darker eyes. He was smiling. Then he began laughing. A girl was screaming beside me. A light flashed and the man was gone. Everything was gone.

I was lying on the ground. My hand hurt. I had dropped what I was holding. Two bronze wedges lay at my side. Nevix was standing over me, holding her walking stick. She was staring at the body on the ground nearby. She hobbled over and poked it with her stick. There was no movement. She tried again, harder this time but the body still didn't move.

I got up and walked over to the body. I looked at Nevix. She nodded. I knelt down and placed my hands on the body's shoulders. I looked up at Nevix. She nodded again. Slowly I began to turn the body over. My sister knelt down and helped me. I felt for a pulse but I couldn't find one. I knelt over and listened for breath. There was none. The man in the darkness was dead.

I pulled the body by the ankles, away from the trees and into the moonlight. A pale face looked up at us. It was Therorb – the old chief whose disappearance had made way for Rindelf's father to take over. Thereob's eyes were black and still. Blood oozed from a thick gash on the side of his head.

Before either of us could speak we heard

the sound of footsteps on the path. A tall figure stepped out from the trees into the moonlight. It was the Foreseer. He looked at us and then to the body on the ground. His face went as pale as the moon. He fell to his knees beside the body. He looked at Nevix and the stick she was carrying.

"It wasn't me," she said. "I didn't kill him."

The Foreseer turned to look at me. He saw the blood on my hands.

"Neither did I," I spluttered. "He hit his head on a branch as he was running away from me."

The Foreseer wrapped his hand in cloth and picked up the two bronze wedges.

"Do you think Therob was taking the bronze wedges back to the Beaker people?" Nevix asked.

The Foreseer didn't answer. He picked up the old chief and slung him over his shoulder. Slowly and without saying a word, the Foreseer carried the body back to his house.

Chapter 10

The Foreseer was different after that night in the woods. He didn't want to speak to me. He didn't even want to look at me. I think he blamed me for Therorb's death. He spent much of his time away, helping prepare the funeral. When he was at home, he would sit outside and stare into the fire or up into the sky. Many people gathered for the funeral. They were there more for the Foreseer than for their old chief. We waited outside the stone circle for the funeral procession to arrive. The sun was setting behind us as we watched the crowd slowly move along the avenue.

We heard Ecron before we could see her. She was crying and shouting words about her old chief. Priests walked beside her. They were dressed in dark furs like Ecron. Each of the three priests carried a small pot of burning incense.

Four men lifted the chief towards us. The Foreseer was at the front. The former chief's body was wrapped in linen cloth and flowers. Many women walked behind the former chief carrying some of his most valuable possessions.

We moved over to the burial mounds behind the avenue. The men carried the body towards us. I walked up onto the wooden platform, along with many others and looked down into the deep hole. The men carefully lowered the body to the ground.

The Foreseer slowly lowered the body into the hole and then curled it up tight. The four women lifted the objects up towards the sky. The large red sun made the gold glow. They took turns placing the objects around the chief. Bones, tools and axes went in first, then knives, daggers and a shield. The chief's golden chest-plate and jewellery followed. Finally, the women added three beautifully decorated pots, each of them full of food.

"It's so sad," my sister whispered. "What a waste of beautiful jewellery."

I climbed down from the viewing platform on the wooden ladder and stood around the grave. A few others joined me but most walked away. The Foreseer began to shovel dirt onto the body as the light disappeared. There were tears in his eyes.

With the burial over the party could begin. There was a new moon for a new chief, and the villagers danced happily beneath it. The air was soon full of the smell of roasting meats.

Veronus sat on a huge chair upon a raised platform. Under the full moon, his golden jewellery sparkled with stars. Rindef and his sister stood beside him. They looked so proud. They smiled at the people dancing and eating. For just about everyone, this was a night to celebrate.

The Foreseer wasn't celebrating through. He wasn't even eating or drinking. He was carving marks onto his wooden staff with his tiny copper knife. He was staring up into the stars, not at his knife. He cut his finger and blood began to trickle down the staff. He only noticed when Rindef whispered to him.

"Tell your father I'll be over in a minute," he said. Nevix tore a strip from her dress and stood up. She steadied herself with her stick and then bandaged his finger.

"Thank you," he said softly, without looking at her. "I'll be back soon enough."

We watched the two men talking. All around

them, people were singing and dancing, smiling and laughing. Their conversation soon turned into an argument. When the chief shouted, he seemed to be looking towards us. My sister, Rindef and I tried to guess what they were talking about. Finally, the two men said goodbye to each other and ended their meeting with a handshake. The Foreseer looked happier than the chief.

I was desperate to find out what they had been talking about. We had to wait until we were alone, on the walk back to the house, to find out.

"The building starts tomorrow," the Foreseer said.

Rebuilding the stone circle, the day after a feast, wasn't a popular decision. Only a few people were stood beneath the rising sun. Those that were there were shielding their eyes from the sun and grumbling to each other. Slowly, more people began to trudge along the avenue.

"At this rate, it will take us twenty years to get you home," the Foreseer said. It wasn't what I wanted to hear.

Soon enough people had gathered and the Foreseer told them what they had to do. He pointed at people and they groaned back at him. They stopped complaining when he waved his staff to the sun. The villagers: men, women and older children, began to disappear in small groups to start their jobs. Some carried their tools towards the forests and others, mostly the women, returned to the village. A few of the older children stayed near the stone circle and began to pick up small stones and pull wild flowers. My sister and I began to help them.

"No you don't," the Foreseer said to me, "you're coming with me."

"What about me?" my sister said, looking up at the Foreseer.

"Sorry," he said. "You'll just slow us down."

My sister's face went red.

"Don't throw that stone at me," the Foreseer said to her, "you'll only have to pick it up again."

He turned his back on her and walked away. I walked with him. I could hear my sister mumbling under her breath.

"There is a flip side to everything," the Foreseer said to me. "You and your sister need to remember that."

Chapter 11

The Foreseer and I walked for some time, mostly in silence. We moved through the village and beyond it, past his house and into the woods behind. The Forseer stopped at a spot where bunches of flowers had been laid on the ground. They marked the spot where Therorb had died. He stood and stared for a moment and then began to walk again.

The woods became thicker and darker the further we went. Just when my legs were beginning to ache, I saw thin smoke spirals above the trees. Then I smelt the most amazing smell.

In the middle of the forest in a clearing stood a small square building surrounded by tall hazel trees. Walls covered three parts of the house, but the other side was open. A fire crackled inside. I felt its heat before I saw it.

We looked into the open room. Flames were licking the blackened walls. The fire spat amber sparks, which floated on the black smoke. Some landed on the straw covered floor. A small ball of fire began to sizzle and smoke.

"Tremel," the Foreseer shouted. "Tremel!" The Foreseer walked into the room, picked up a bucket of water and threw it into the smoke. There was a scream, then coughing. A man's voice shouted.

A pair of wide, white eyes came out of the fading smoke. I could see streaks of reddish skin on his face between the black smoke stains. He stamped on the ground to kill the fire. The Foreseer began to laugh loudly.

"What are you doing here?" said the man. He spoke the Lowlander's language, but slower than most. I found it easy to understand him.

"I've come to see how you're getting on," the Foreseer replied. "And it's a good job we did. You were about to smelt yourself."

"I wasn't asleep," the man said, I was just resting my eyes. He smiled. His teeth were almost as black as the rest of his face.

He held out a small, clay container in his green stained fingers. It was the same shape and size as the bronze wedge. There were many marks and grooves carved into it.

"An excellent mould," the Foreseer said.

"It will do the job," the man replied.

The Foreseer turned to me. "Where are my manners. Harocu – this is Tremel – the best bronze smith there is. He can make anything out of bronze."

"Or copper," Tremel added.

Tremel handed me the mould. I looked at the red scars and blisters that covered his arms.

"You can try smelting, if you like," he said.

I looked at his arms again. "No thanks," I said, weakly, handing him the mould back.

We followed Tremel outside, to the back of the house. The Foreseer and I stood around a deep pit and watched Tremel fill half of it with charcoal. He then sprinkled green powder over the charcoal. The Foreseer began to knock two pieces of sharp flint together. Small sparks began to fly from them. Tremel caught a spark in a small ball of hay.

"Blow softly," he whispered.

When I blew, the hay caught fire. Carefully, Tremel lowered the smoking ball into the charcoal pit and then poked it with a long stick to spread the flames. He and the Foreseer lifted a huge lid of moist dirt, with a hole in its middle and lowered it onto the pit. Tremel walked over carrying a strange looking object – a bag with a pipe sticking out of it.

"It's called a bellows," the Foreseer said.

Tremel stuck the pipe of the bellows onto the end of a long, clay pipe that poked out of the ground. He then began to pump it. He pulled the handles apart and the bag filled with air. Then he squeezed the handles together and pushed the air out. Red and white sparks burst out of the hole in the dirt lid. Every time Tremel pumped, the sparks shot higher.

"That looks like hard work," I said to the Foreseer.

"It is," he said. "That's why you're going to do it."

I took the bellows from Tremel and started to pump air, making the sparks fly. It felt good.

"How long do I have to keep this up?" I asked.

The two men laughed. "Just a few hours," the Foreseer said. It didn't feel so good anymore.

"We're off for a drink," the Foreseer said. "Watching you is thirsty work. Keep on going."

The Foreseer and Tremel walked away. I could

hear them laughing inside the house. Sweat was trickling down my head and my arms were beginning to ache.

"Didn't think we were going to leave you, did you?" the Foreseer shouted, as he walked back to me. "We'll be here forever if we leave it to you." Tremel took over the pumping and the sparks began to fly again.

"Hungry?" the Foreseer asked. I followed him into the house.

"Tremel has baked us some bread," he said. He handed me a large, warm hunk of bread. It had green powder around the edges.

"Don't worry – it's not mould," he said. "Just powdered rock."

We walked over to the edge of the forest and sat with our backs against a tree. The Foreseer took the bread from me. He took out his small, copper knife and cut away the green bits.

"Tremel's a better smith than baker," the Foreseer said.

We chewed in silence for some time and watched the sparks shooting out of the lid.

I was tired. Working the bellows in the midday sun had made me sleepy.

I was woken by a kick to my leg. The Foreseer was looking down at me. Tremel was beside him, carrying a large beaker.

"Thirsty?" the Foreseer asked.

I nodded and began to drink. The Foreseer was staring at something behind me.

"What is it?" I whispered.

He put a finger to his lips. His eyes were still peering into the woods behind me. Finally, he looked down at me and smiled.

"I thought I saw something moving in the woods. It was probably just an animal. Maybe it could smell the bread. Now come on, get up. Tremel has a job for you."

"Great," I puffed. I pushed myself up with my aching arms. I followed the two men back to the pit. Tremel lifted the lid. There were no sparks, just thin grey smoke clouds floating on the breeze.

The Foreseer picked up a tool with a short, wooden handle and a wide blade of animal bone at the end. He began to dig the charcoal with it.

"Made it myself," he said, proudly, as he scraped the charcoal with his shovel. Grey smoke puffed into the air. Tremel poked the charcoal with a stick. He pushed some small black rocks into a bowl. When he poured water into the bowl the black rocks hissed at him.

When he swirled the water around the bowl something amazing happened. Some of the rocks had changed from black to yellow. Tremel picked them up and threw the black rocks away.

"Copper," the Foreseer said. "See if you can find some more."

Tremel dropped more small rocks into the bowl and added water. I moved the bowl. Small, yellow rocks began to glow beneath the water. My smile was as wide as the bowl.

"Wonderful, isn't it?" the Foreseer said. "But the best bit is still to come."

Tremel carried the copper chunks back inside the house. A small, round clay pot, with a long handle, was smoking on a huge black bed of charcoal. Tremel quickly turned the charcoal with his stick. The heat burnt my face and made my eyes water. Tremel wrapped one hand in a huge, fur-lined glove and lifted the pot. He dropped the copper rocks in, along with a chunk of tin and returned the pot to the furnace.

We waited a few minutes. What I saw next

was magical. Tremel lifted the pot again. The copper chunks had melted and were swimming inside the pot. It looked like Tremel had melted a bit of the sun. The Foreseer brought over a large wooden bowl, half filled with water. He placed the wedge mould into it and put the bowl on the table. Slowly, Tremel poured the shiny amber liquid into the mould. The melted bronze hissed and steam burst from the mould. The Foreseer and I left the mould to cool and crushed more green rock.

Now seemed a good time to ask the Foreseer the question I had wanted to ask for ages: "Why do we need the Bronze Sun, to get back?" He didn't look at me and carried on grinding.

"Because it got you here," he finally said. "It got us both here."

"What do you mean?" I said.

He put his grinding stone down. I did the same.

"I can't really remember," he said. "When I touch a wedge, I see glimpses of what happened. Images and faces. I haven't looked back for some time now. I don't want to remember anymore."

I couldn't believe it. He saw the images too.

"The same thing happens to me," I said. "I have seen images and faces."

The Foreseer didn't look surprised. "You see what I saw," he said. "Same room. Same face."

"What room, what face?" I shouted.

Tremel walked in. He was carrying a small parcel, wrapped in cloth. He knelt down and carefully peeled the cloth back. The bronze wedge looked incredible. The Foreseer held the cloth and lifted the wedge. He turned it over to examine both sides.

"Incredible," he said. "It looks and feels exactly the same. The markings are perfect."

Tremel returned with a leather bag over his shoulder. He knelt again and lifted another cloth wrapped parcel from the bag. The other two wedges were under the cloth.

"Now it's time to see just how good you are," the Foreseer said to Tremel.

The Foreseer wrapped his hands in cloth and began to piece the wedges together. Slowly he placed the new piece between the two old wedges. The three bronze wedges were joined together to make a perfect circle. A Bronze Sun.

A huge smile filled the Foreseer's face. "You're

almost home," he said.

"You mean, *we're* almost home," I said. "You're going back too, aren't you?"

"Of course," he said, still smiling.

We left Tremel's workshop and returned a different way. After hours of walking we stopped and rested by a small clump of trees in the middle of a field. I had no idea where we were. I sat with my back to a tree.

"This is a good place to do it," he said.

"Do what?" I asked.

The Foreseer wrapped his hand in a cloth and pulled the three wedges from the bag. With great care, he lowered them onto the ground and placed them together to form the circle again.

"We're going to hold the Bronze Sun," he said.

I didn't speak. My mouth was locked by shock.

"Haven't you wondered what will happen if we touch all three pieces?" he said.

I had – ever since I had seen the three pieces together.

"I thought you didn't want to remember anymore," I said.

"I didn't want to see the flashing images again," he began. "But maybe, with the three pieces together, I'll see what really happened. Don't you want to know how you got here? Don't you want to know where you are from?"

Of course I wanted to know but the thought of knowing scared me. What if I saw something terrible? I began to think I might be better off not knowing.

The Foreseer took the cloth off his hands.

"Ready?" he said.

My fingers were shaking. My heart was thumping hard.

"On my count of three, we'll touch the circle together," the Foreseer said.

I nodded. I closed my eyes tight. I took a deep breath.

"One…Two…Three…"

I gripped the Bronze Sun tightly. A huge force shook me.

I was in the room again. I was trapped inside a glass cage. My sister stood in a cage opposite me. There was a huge, shiny frame around her. There was a circle of shiny frames. There were empty cages beneath the other frames. I looked up. I was under one too. It looked just like the circle of stones. An object stood in the centre of the circle, between my sister and me. It was a Bronze Sun. Light bounced off its polished surface.

A pale face moved in front of me. Dark, cold eyes stared into me. He blew against the glass wall of the cage. His face was lost in a cloud of steam. I saw his finger moving. He was writing on the window.

Bring it back.

His hand moved across the window. The words were gone but his face was there. Then he walked away. My sister was staring at me. She looked scared. A huge, grinding sound made me look up. The roof was moving. Rays of light shot into the room. The Bronze Sun sparkled. Light bounced off it and turned the frames white. My sister's cage began to glow brighter and brighter. The light found me. It got hotter and hotter inside the cage. A dazzling flash blinded me. The room was gone.

I was lying on the grass. The Foreseer was sitting up. He was holding the wedges close to his chest in his wrapped hands. All the colour had been sucked from his face. He was staring. Not at me though. He was staring at the hundreds of Beaker people who stood in a huge circle. Each of them was holding some type of weapon. I looked up at bronze daggers and axes, stone hammers and maces. I wished I was back in the white room again.

Chapter 12

The Foreseer put his arm on my shoulder. A girl, no older than me, stepped forward.

"We've been following you," she said.

"And now you've got us," the Foreseer said. "Don't kill the boy. It's me and the Bronze Sun you want."

She laughed. So did many of her people.

"No it isn't," she said. "We haven't come to kill you. We've come to help you. We want to rebuild the circle and end this war between our people."

The Foreseer laughed so much he fell onto his back.

"I didn't see that coming," he said. "Harocu, meet Defrin. She's the Beaker chief's daughter."

Defrin whistled. More of her people came out of the woods. They brought horses with them. Defrin offered the Foreseer a large, chestnut horse. Every time he tried to climb up, the horse moved. Every time the horse moved, the Beaker people laughed. Finally, with the help of two men who held the horse, he climbed on top. A huge cheer startled the horse and threw the Foreseer forward. He hung on, upside down, with his arms wrapped tightly around the horse's neck. Some of the Beaker people laughed so much that tears streaked down their dirty faces.

Defrin helped him. She pulled him round and then whispered to the horse. Her voice was soft and soothing. She wore the most incredible fur coat – a patchwork of blacks and browns that fluttered behind her when she rode.

The air was thick and sticky and a distant rumble told me that a storm was coming. We rode quicker. The people had to run to keep up.

It was dark by the time we reached the village. Men, carrying spears and torches, stood guarding the entrance.

Veronus rode out to meet Defrin and the Foreseer with two warriors walking on either side of him. They pointed their spears towards Defrin who rode back to her people and spoke to them. She then led her people towards our village. The light of the moon caught her head. Her black hair shone like wet crow feathers. The tiny blue beads around her neck twinkled with the stars.

The Lowland warriors stood to one side as Defrin led her Beakers through the tunnel of light into the village. Our people stared at the Beakers and whispered to each other. Mother's held their children tighter. Warriors clutched their spears. The sky rumbled again.

We all stopped in the heart of the village. The Beaker people stood together, watched by the suspicious Lowlanders. The Foreseer stood on a wooden platform and looked down on the large crowd.

He explained why the Beaker people were here and urged our people to welcome them into the village. He said we needed their help. We couldn't rebuild the circle without them. Mutters and moans spread amongst the villagers. They didn't trust the Beaker people; they didn't want them in their village. The Foreseer looked worried. His words weren't working.

He told the crowd that the gods wanted the two tribes to work together. The fighting had angered the gods and it had to stop. The villagers didn't believe him. The Foreseer called Defrin to join him. This made things worse. The crowd began to jeer and shout when she walked onto the platform. Her people moved forward, holding their tools as weapons.

The jeering was so loud that I couldn't hear what she said. The villagers were screaming at Defrin and her people were shouting back at them. Even the sky was angry. It rumbled above us. The Foreseer whispered in Defrin's ear. She nodded and he handed her his shoulder bag.

As she fumbled in the bag the crowd below were boiling with anger. Some were trying to get past the guards to climb onto the platform. Defrin lifted something high above her head. In the darkness, the crowd couldn't see what it was and continued shouting and screaming. An incredible crack of lightning cut through the air. The lightening lit the Bronze Sun that Defrin held. Another fork of lightening stabbed the sky and silenced the crowd.

The Foreseer spoke again and this time the people listened. He told them that the gods were angry. This time the crowd believed him. A mother and child walked from the crowd of villagers towards the Beaker people. She held out her hand towards a Beaker woman and her child and led them back to her home. Others followed. Soon, all the Beaker people had left with a villager.

Defrin came with us. We reached the Foreseer's house just before the rain. We sat inside around the fire, eating meat and berries. Defrin and the Foreseer drank a honey drink from a large jug. They burst out laughing when my sister hobbled into the house. I did too.

She looked like she had been swimming in white paint. The rain had soaked her clothes and spread white chalk all over her. Her hair covered most of her face and dripped chalky white water on the floor. When she pulled her hair from her face, we could see how angry she was.

"Where have you two been?" she shouted. "Had a nice day out, have you!"

The Foreseer and I looked at each other. Both of us were too scared to speak. She shook her hands, wetting us with chalky water. There was another storm coming and this one was going to be inside the house.

"And who's your new girlfriend," she hissed at me.

"Her name is Defrin," the Foreseer said. "She's

a Beaker."

My sister took a deep breath.

"A Beaker girl…in our house! After what they did to me! Are you mad?"

By now, she was frothing at the mouth.

"Why is she in our house?" she demanded.

I looked at the Foreseer and shook my head, silently telling him to say no more. He understood and stayed silent.

"I'm Defrin: the chief's daughter. It's nice to meet you," she said.

For a moment, Nevix didn't move. I held my breath and waited. Her mouth dropped open. The storm was coming.

"Nice to meet you! Are you serious? Your people threw stones at me. Your father was going to kill me! It's not nice to meet you!"

Parts of her face were white but most were now blood red. She was a terrifying sight.

"I was only trying to be friendly," Defrin said. "But you're right. My father's men treated you horribly. I had nothing to do with that. Our women want peace."

I didn't think that Nevix could look any angrier but she could.

"Here, take my coat, you look like you need it more than me," Defrin said.

My sister snatched the coat from Defrin's hand, threw it to the floor and stamped white footprints all over it.

"I don't want anything from you," she screamed. She stormed past us, slamming the woven door to her 'room' behind her.

"That went better than I expected," the Foreseer said.

Nevix appeared again. She pushed the fence open and picked up the coat. She began to wipe the white footprints off. She didn't look up once. She turned, walked back into her room and calmly closed the fence behind her.

I looked at the Foreseer and Defrin. Like me, they were biting their lips, trying not to laugh.

"So she did want something from me," Defrin chuckled.

My sister didn't join us around the fire even though she needed it more than us. Defrin waited until she was sure Nevix was asleep before she went into her room. I stood up to go to bed but the Foreseer stopped me.

"Sit down," he said. "We have a lot to talk

about."

It had been a long day. I wanted sleep not conversation.

"Tell me what you saw when you held the Bronze Sun," the Foreseer said. "I need to know what you saw."

I followed him into the side room.

"Draw everything you remember," he said, handing me a sharpened twig. "Try to draw it exactly how you saw it. If you can't remember, you could hold the sun again."

"I can remember," I said.

I began to scratch a picture into the dirt showing the circle of glass cases and the shiny frames that I'd seen in my vision. The Foreseer was very interested. He asked me about their size and the distance between them. I didn't know for sure. I could only guess.

"We need to get the stone circle right," he said. "We need to make it look as close to what you saw as possible if we're to get you back."

I felt very nervous. "What will happen if we don't get it right?" I asked him.

"We will get it right – if your memory is accurate," he insisted.

Now I was feeling really scared.

"We've got less than 60 rises of the sun, to rebuild the stone circle," he said.

"Why do we have to have it finished by then?" I asked him.

"That's the longest day," he said. "The day the sun shines the longest and the strongest. The power of the two suns will unite to send you home."

"We can do that, can't we?" I asked him, "now that the Beaker people are going to help us."

The Foreseer now looked very serious. He had his hands gripped tightly together.

"There is a problem," he said. He paused before he continued. "Not all the Beaker people want to help us. Defrin told me that her father, Zerban, is gathering thousands of his people, from across the waters, to march on us to reclaim the Bronze Sun. When he returns, he will lead the largest army this land has ever seen."

Chapter 13

Every morning we walked to the stones at first light. We gathered in the circle and the Foreseer told us what we had to do. He placed us into groups. People were matched to jobs: the strongest (mostly men but some Beaker women too) were the lifters, the diggers and pullers.

Those who weren't as strong, like Rindef, Defrin and me, collected wood and built with it. We had a few carpenters in the group and we quickly learnt from them.

Our worst job was digging out the chalk circle. Half of the chalk went all over me and the other half I swallowed. I had no idea why the Foreseer wanted the circle dug even deeper.

The weakest people: our women, young children and the old men, reshaped the stones. They spent their days chipping and polishing, knocking small balls of stone against large blocks of stone. Nevix hated it. She said that as soon as her leg was better, she would join our group.

It wasn't long before she was able to walk without her stick. Nevix helped collect wood and build the huge towers and bridges. Soon she was carrying more wood and moving it faster than anyone else. She and Defrin quickly became friends and were always talking together.

The stone circle united the people. Beakers and villagers worked together, talked together, ate together and laughed together. Beakers helped the villagers and the villagers helped the people. However, I knew there were many Beaker people who wanted war – not peace. I knew that we were in a race against time.

Some of the tallest sarsen stones had fallen forward and some lay flat on the ground. My group stopped working to watch hundreds of men and a few women trying to move them. They had dug a huge hole in the ground and placed a giant tree trunk into the hole with two ropes tied around it. They then tied the end of one rope around a flat sarsen stone. A small group stood around the huge stone, holding long, sharpened, wooden stakes.

Another rope dangled from the top of the tree trunk. About thirty people grabbed the loose rope. As they pulled on it, I held my breath. The huge wooden lever began to creak. The stone wobbled. Men shouted. More joined them. They pulled again. They groaned. The stone groaned and wobbled. Then it began to lift at the front. The group squeezed the wooden stakes under the stone. The stone fell back and the lifters sighed in relief.

The workers could pull the stones now they had rollers under them. Lifting them up, into position, was much harder. For days, many workers dug deep holes in the ground. The strongest men and women pulled the stones and left them hanging over the holes. Others lifted the huge tree trunk into position, from the other side behind the deep hole.

The Foreseer tied the rope from the tree trunk around the huge stone. When he gave the signal, about a hundred workers pulled on the rope. It took many tries and many days for the workers to lift all the stones into position. The Foreseer was hard to please. Several times, he said that the stones were not at the right height or at the right angle so they had to be lowered and lifted again. When the stone was in the right position, we would fill the gaps around it with mud, chalk and rocks to keep it steady.

Lifting the curved stone tops (or lintels) onto the upright stones, was even harder. Only the strongest men could do it. They stood on the huge wooden frame then levered and pulled the stone up towards them. When it was high enough, people below slid huge wooden planks under it. When the stone was steady and the men were ready, they pulled again.

It took hours to raise each stone. When it reached the top of the frame, work stopped and everyone came to look. The men pushed the lintel onto the platform, which was level with the top of the stones. Slowly they pushed the lintel forward until it locked into position on top. This took hours.

When the men locked the last of the lintels into position, a cheer shook the dark sky.

We sat down and admired our work. Five huge stone frames (the Foreseer called them trilithons) now stood in a horseshoe shape. They were inside a circle of smaller sarsen stones. Each one had a lintel roof lying flat on top. There was a circle of polished bluestones between the circle of sarsen stones and the huge stone door frames.

That night we celebrated. The Beaker people and villagers ate, drank and danced together. Everyone was happy, even Nevix. She climbed the wooden frame to the very top and stood on the stone circle. The crowd cheered as she ran around the stone roof. The crowd cheered even louder when Defrin climbed the frame to join her. The two girls ran, holding each other's hands on top of the circle of stones.

The feast would have gone on all night if the Foreseer hadn't stopped it. He wanted everyone to rest. We followed him home. He sent Defrin to bed and then spoke to us about the next day. He told us what we had to do. It took ages to get to sleep. I couldn't stop thinking about tomorrow. Would I be going home? Where was home?

I was shaken awake. Defrin's face glowed beneath her torch. My sister groaned when we woke her. The sky was black. All was quiet. Even the birds were still sleeping.

As we walked through the village, we drank water and ate berries. Dark shapes walked ahead of us. A line of flames stretched towards the stone circle. When we reached the avenue, the sky was beginning to lighten. Blue lines cut through the blackness. Morning was coming.

Warriors stood on both sides of the avenue. Armed Beaker people alongside armed villagers. Defrin left us to speak to them. Four men stood with torches at the top of the wooden frame, each one looking out in a different direction.

The Foreseer walked out from the circle to greet us. He held a torch in one hand and his mace in the other.

"Are you expecting trouble?" I asked him. He didn't answer.

"Look at this," he said.

He led us past the stones, many of which the villagers had covered in flowers, into the centre of the circle. He stood beside the altar stone. A long wooden pole stuck out of the stone. The Bronze Sun was on the top.

"You remember what you need to do?" the Foreseer said.

Nevix and I both nodded.

The Foreseer was staring at the Bronze Sun. He turned to look at us. His face was as white as the chalk in the circle.

"Get to your positions," he said.

"Will you get to yours?" I asked.

"No. Not yet," he replied as he looked up at the sky. "We have to hold them. To give you time."

"You mean give *us* time," said my sister.

"Of course," he said, smiling.

He walked quickly to join the chief. Veronus sat high up on his horse, looking out towards the avenue.

The men on top of the frame shouted. The Bronze Sun was shaking. The ground was jumping. We could feel the Beaker Army approaching: the beat of their drums; the thudding of feet and hooves on the ground. Our villagers – who had come to watch the sunrise – began to panic and ran inside the circle. Our warriors who had come to fight ran out to meet the enemy.

My sister began to walk away.

"Where are you going Nevix?" I asked.

"To fight," she said.

"But you can't," I shouted, grabbing her arm. "We need to be ready for the sunrise. When the sun strikes the Bronze Sun we must be under a stone frame."

She stared at me. Even in the gloom, I could

see the fire in her eyes.

"I won't let these people die for me. I have to fight. The sun isn't up yet. If we don't fight, we might be dead before dawn."

I knew there was no point arguing. I hadn't known my sister for long – not in this world anyway – but I knew her well enough to realise that arguing with her was a waste of time. She ran off, snatching a sword from a passing warrior. I followed her. I wanted to stay close to her.

I could now see the Beaker Army. A huge black shape marching towards us, under the purple sky. A strip of orange glowed bright behind them. They were going to reach the circle before the sun.

Chapter 14

Our warriors ran to defend the stone circle. They stood outside the ditch. The archers pushed their way to the front. When the command came, hundreds of arrows flew towards the advancing army. Shouts and cries filled the air.

The Beaker army then split into three. One part stayed but the other two went in different directions. Soon they surrounded us. They stood ten deep around the circle. We had one line with huge gaps between the warriors. Defrin and Rindef stood in the circle. My sister and I joined them.

A huge scream moved around the Beaker lines. Then they showed us how they were going to kill us, brandishing their bronze long-swords and stone axes. I turned back to look at Veronus. He looked terrified.

The Beaker army ran and rode towards us. Their charge shook the ground and their screams shook the sky. The villagers inside the circle were screaming too. Defrin and Nevix moved forward to fight but a huge blast on a horn stopped them. The horn kept blasting. It was coming from behind us. It was coming from the top of the tower.

We turned and ran over the wooden bridges. When we were inside the circle, we pulled the bridges toward us, away from the ditch. Men shouted from the top of the tower. The warriors around me lifted up the bridge and we hid behind it. Arrows thudded into our wooden wall.

I looked up to see flaming arrows lighting up the sky. The men on top of the tower were firing but their arrows were falling into the ditch, short of their target.

I was wrong. The ditch was the target. It burst into flames. Soon we were hiding behind a circle of fire. Our people cheered. Their people shouted. Their horses panicked and stopped.

I peered out from behind the wooden wall. I could see the Beaker warriors through the smoke and gaps in the flames. Their faces were as red as the flames. They were holding their weapons ready to charge. The fire couldn't protect us forever.

The sun was rising. A huge golden arc rose like a rainbow into the purple sky.

"We have to go," I shouted to Nevix.

She didn't want to move. She wanted to fight. I grabbed her arm and pulled her towards the stones. The screaming behind us made us stop and turn.

A small group of Beaker warriors were charging towards the wall of fire. They were carrying long spears in one hand and axes in the other. I couldn't believe they were running at the fire! I stood with my mouth open as they stuck their spears into the ground and flew over the flames.

They swung their axes as they fell. Our warriors came out from behind their walls to meet them. The air rattled with the sound of weapon on weapon and the screams of the wounded.

Many Beakers fell to the ground but more continued to drop over the flames. Two tall shadows stood on top of a wooden wall, knocking our people to the ground with their axes. They seemed to be staring at us. They jumped and landed in the glow of the sun.

"Raktes and Zerban," my sister hissed. "They

want the Bronze Sun. If they want it, they will have to come and get it."

She pulled the wooden pole from the altar stone and ran towards the wooden frame.

"Stay by the altar stone," she shouted to me. I was too shocked to argue.

She climbed up the tall tower and stood on top, waving the pole. Raktes and Zerban saw the Bronze Sun on the end of it and screamed at Nevix. Raktes pulled his way up towards the top of the tower. His father followed. The men on top leant over and fired their arrows down towards them. All missed. Zerban turned around and shouted to his warriors. Arrows flew over his head and into the men on top of the tower. Only one man wasn't hit. The Foreseer stood beside Nevix holding his mace.

The Beaker army had pushed our warriors back. The fighting was now at the edge of the stone circle. Soon the battle would be lost.

Raktes was almost at the top of the tower. My sister kicked his hand. He pulled his hand away but grabbed her leg, pulling her down towards him. She punched him hard in the face and he fell back, saving himself by clutching onto the wooden frame.

Nevix and the Foreseer jumped from the tower onto the top of the stone door frames.

"Come and get it," she shouted, waving the pole with the Bronze Sun on its end. Raktes, and then his father, Zerban stood on top of the tower. They jumped and landed on the flat stones. Their shadows shimmered above the rising sun. Light was beginning to seep into the circle.

Zerban and Raktes split up and came at us brandishing their weapons. Zerban walked around the stone roof towards the Foreseer and Raktes walked towards Nevix.

Raktes swung his axe. Nevix jumped over it and hit him with the end of the pole. He stumbled back before advancing again. Zerban twirled his mace as he moved forward towards the Foreseer. The Foreseer edged backwards. So did Nevix. They stood back-to-back, ready to fight.

I could see the sun rising through the stone frames. Its light had reached many of the villagers who were huddled together inside the stone circle. The fighting continued around them and above them.

Nevix was using the pole to keep Raktes' axe

away from her. He couldn't get close enough to strike her. Every time he swung the axe, she moved out of the way and whacked him with the pole. But try as she might, she couldn't hit the giant hard enough to knock him off the stone rooftop.

Zerban and the Foreseer fought with maces. One hit, the other blocked. One pushed forward – the other pushed back.

Raktes swung his huge axe again. My sister jumped to avoid it but wobbled on the curved lintel as she landed. As the Bronze Sun and pole fell she screamed my name. I ran and caught the pole and placed it back in the altar stone. The rays of the sun were stretching out towards it. The Beaker warriors behind me were fighting their way towards it.

My sister and the Foreseer were back-to-back. She threw punches and kicked Raktes but he kept moving towards her. He lifted his huge axe high into the air and it began to fall towards her.

Zerban swung his mace towards the Foreseer's head but the Foreseer ducked beneath the blow and it hit Raktes. Raktes fell flat on his face. His axe dropped to the ground.

"Go," shouted the Foreseer.

"I can't leave you," Nevix screamed back at him.

"You must, or people have died for nothing. Go!" I had never seen him angry before. He began to push Zerban back.

Nevix jumped over Raktes and leapt onto the wooden tower. Zerban shouted at his warriors. The arrows came again, thudding into the wood around Nevix. The arrows kept coming. She continued to climb down, placing her hands on the arrow shafts.

The huge red sun hung in the sky. Its rays were breaking into the circle through the gaps in the stones. They reached out over the altar stone like golden fingers.

Nevix jumped from the tower and landed in a heap. Defrin ran out to help her. She lifted her from the ground and pulled her beneath a stone frame. I ran and took my place.

The rays of light were creeping up the pole towards the Bronze Sun. The light spread over the stone frames and turned them bronze too. The shadows continued fighting above us. The Foreseer was pushing the Beaker chief back. He screamed at his warriors to help him.

The Beaker army was so close now. I could smell the blood on their axes. I could hear their grunts and groans. I could hear the screams of pain they left behind. Then everything fell silent. The screaming stopped. The fighting stopped. The Foreseer looked down at us.

"You go, I stay," he shouted. "Remember – there's always a flip side."

The Bronze Sun was glowing. The light had reached it. It glowed brighter and brighter. A column of the brightest light burst from it and lit up a stone frame. Then another came. The third shone onto my sister's stone frame and the fourth came towards me. I covered my eyes to shield them from the blinding light. I looked to the floor to see a fifth light burst forward. Then all lights seemed to join as one. They span together, faster and faster and then burst into an incredible flash.

Chapter 15

When I opened my eyes the blinding light had gone. The stone circle and all the people inside it had disappeared. My sister stood opposite me. Like me she was trapped inside a hot glass box which glowed beneath a shining white door frame. Moments later the glass doors clicked and slid open.

"Welcome back. Please walk out of your transporter." The man's deep voice echoed around the room. It seemed to be coming from everywhere and nowhere.

We walked out and stood together next to a silver display panel. We were inside a circle of five shining door frames, each with a glass box beneath. We both stared at the same glass box – the one with Defrin inside.

"How did she get here! I never saw her in my visions," I gasped.

"Me neither," my sister said.

I looked at Defrin again. Her door was open

but she was still inside. She looked terrified. She was shaking and her eyes and her mouth were wide open. My sister walked up to the glass cage and pulled the startled girl from it.

"I couldn't stay," said Defrin in a shaky voice. She was talking to us but her eyes were scanning the room.

"Not after I had betrayed my father and brother. I could never go back to them. They'd kill me," Defrin explained.

"They might be dead themselves," I said.

Defrin looked to the floor. My sister put an arm around her shoulder. The deep voice spoke again.

"I see you've brought a friend back," said the voice.

I turned. The smiling man had the darkest eyes I had ever seen. He wore a shiny black cloak. I looked at my sister. I could tell from her expression that she had seen this man before.

"So which one of you has it?" he said sweetly.

I looked at Nevix and Defrin. Like me, they didn't understand what he was talking about. I looked back at the man. His smile had gone.

"The Bronze Sun, of course," he said. There

was anger in his voice. "You were meant to be touching it. It should have come back with you."

I looked at my sister. She didn't want to speak. I told him what happened. I told him how we got back when the sun's rays had hit the Bronze Sun and activated the stone circle.

The smile briefly returned to the man's face. "They did it. They really did. Incredible."

Then the smile went again. "They want the Bronze Sun for themselves. They want to keep it where they think I can't get it," he snarled. "Well, they're wrong. I've waited over thirty years for it. They're not keeping it."

His sharp voice scared me. My sister, however, had found her courage.

"Why do you want the Bronze Sun?" she asked.

He clapped. A tall, thin woman walked forward wearing the same black suit as her master. She was carrying a round object. It was a another Bronze Sun.

The man took it from her. "I made this copy from one of the original pieces. But I want the Bronze Sun to be whole again," he said.

"Why?" I asked him.

He looked surprised. "Why? You've forgotten,

haven't you? The time travelling must have messed up your memories. You have forgotten who I am. You don't even know who you are, do you?"

He laughed again, an evil, cold laugh.

"I'm the Curator of *Timecast*: the largest museum in the country and soon to be the only museum in the world. The complete Bronze Sun will be so powerful. It will allow time travel anywhere and to anytime. Imagine what valuable objects I could bring back. I can find objects that have been lost to the world forever. I could take objects from the past and in doing so, take them from the present. Other museums will lose all their treasures!"

As he paced around the room, he stroked the Bronze Sun. My sister spoke and he stopped walking.

"Why can't you do that with your Bronze Sun? Why do you need us?" she said.

"My copy only allows children to travel back in time. But the real sun? That will have the power to send anyone forward or back," he said excitedly.

Thoughts ran through my head.

"But why us?" I asked him.

"You don't remember do you?" he said. "You were selected after months of trials. You were the best of all the pairs."

He could tell we didn't understand him. He pointed at my sister.

"Your speed, your strength and most importantly, your incredible ability to learn languages so quickly were the reasons you were chosen," he explained.

My sister smiled and lifted her shoulders. She looked very proud.

"And me?" I asked. "Why was I chosen?"

A wicked grin spread over his pointed face. "Because you're her twin brother. That's why. For some reason, only twins can travel to the same time together."

My sister laughed. I wanted to hit her. The only reason I had been chosen was that I was her twin brother.

"And now you're going to travel back again. To get the Bronze Sun and bring it here," the Curator said.

"No way!" my sister shouted. "I'm never going back!"

The tall woman grabbed Defrin and pulled her away from us and pointed a weapon at her head.

"A new creation of mine," the Curator said. "I could make your friend history."

He touched some controls on a panel and the lights flickered as the device activated.

"We've had an upgrade since you were last here," he chuckled. "Now, grab my Bronze Sun. Hold it this way up."

My sister and I both shook our heads. Defrin shook hers too. The weapon in the tall woman's hand began to vibrate. Nevix put her hand on the Bronze Sun. Her eyes closed and her body began to shake. When I touched it the same thing happened to me.

I could see him. The Foreseer. He was smiling. He was inside the Stone Circle. He was with Zerban and Veronus. The two chiefs were shaking hands. Raktes and Rindef were beside their fathers. Beaker people and our villagers were talking, not fighting. Axes and swords lay on the grass around their feet. Many of the stones had fallen too. There were gaps within the stone circle. The Bronze Sun was still glowing. It had damaged the circle. We had damaged it. The Foreseer turned to look at me.

"There is always a flip side," he said.

I let go of the Bronze Sun. My sister looked at me. She looked terrified. The Curator pressed another button. Beams of light began to tilt towards us.

"Hold the Bronze Sun," the Curator screamed.

My sister and I looked at each other. I knew what we had to do.

"Bring it back or your friend dies," the Curator shouted. I could feel the heat of the light move up my back and onto my arms.

Then I shouted in the language of the villagers. My sister understood.

We stretched our sleeves over our hands, then flipped the Bronze Sun over and held it in the light. Rays of blinding light bounced off the Bronze Sun and filled the room. Then the light was gone together with The Curator and the assisant. We were still in the room. Defrin clapped. She had pushed herself away from the assistant and fallen to the floor before the light had reached her.

My sister laughed.

"How did you know that would happen?" she asked.

"I just had a feeling," I said. "The Foreseer was always saying that everything had a flip side. He must have been saying that for a reason."

"You're not so useless after all," my sister said. "Not for a boy, I mean."

She hugged me. So did Defrin. I looked over their shoulders at the huge room. I was beginning to remember it. There was somewhere I had to go.

I walked past the large, white frames, down a long corridor, towards a room at the end. I wasn't sure where I was walking but I knew which way I had to go.

The corridor led into a huge, square room. There were ancient objects in glass cases and old paintings hanging on three of the white walls. There were small glass screens on the other wall, each with a button beneath. I walked towards the screen furthest to the left. I pressed the button. A beautiful Bronze shield appeared with the date 1550BC under it. I pressed it again. Two names and two faces appeared. Both were young girls of about my age and looking very similar to each other. Twins.

I pressed some more buttons. More objects

appeared with more dates, more names and more pairs of faces. When the Bronze Sun appeared, my heart seemed to stop beating. I stared at the number on the screen: 21.6.1970 BC. It was the same number the Foreseer had chalked onto his wall. My finger shook over the button. I pressed it.

Two faces looked back at me. Two boys' faces. I didn't know who they were at first. Then I looked harder at the one called Edward Forester. His hair was much shorter. His teeth were much whiter. He was much, much younger. But it was definitely the Foreseer.

Then I realised who James was and everything began to make sense. He wasn't identical to the other boy but I could tell they were brothers. It was Therorb. The old chief of the village, who I had watched die in the woods, was the Foreseer's twin brother.

My finger hovered over the button again. I wanted to press it but fear was stopping me. I took a deep breath and pushed the button. The boys' faces disappeared and were replaced by two different faces: me and my sister. At last I knew my real name. I knew my sister's name.

Memories came flooding back.

"What are you doing in here," my sister shouted. I turned around. Defrin was beside her. They were both carrying bags of crisps and fizzy drinks bottles.

"We found a cool snack machine," she said. "It scanned my eyes and gave me what I asked for. Defrin really likes the bubbles."

They walked over to me. I quickly pressed the button until the Bronze Sun was back on the screen. My sister looked at me.

"Press it again," I told her.

She did. She stared hard at the screen.

"The Foreseer and Therorb," she said. I nodded.

"If you press it again Nevix, you'll find out your real name," I told her.

"My real name must be better than Nevix. I hate being named after a stinky old fox!"

I took Defrin's hand and began to pull her away. She took another swig of her fizzy drink. Her eyes were watering.

We had reached the corridor by the time my sister had pressed the button.

"Daisy!" she screamed. "I'm named after a tiny flower!?!"

She ran over to join us. I was laughing. Defrin was bouncing up and down with hiccups. Daisy looked distraught.

"What's the matter Daisy?" I asked her.

"I've changed my mind, I'm sticking with Nevix," she said. "Come on, let's get out of here. I need to find some new clothes. These old rags are history!"